ever,   ind mysen
nodd

D1428189

Also by Cherie Bennett

WILD HEARTS
WILD HEARTS ON FIRE
WILD HEARTS ON THE EDGE

WILD HEARTS Forever

CHERIE BENNETT

**POCKET
BOOKS**

LONDON · SYDNEY · NEW YORK · TOKYO · SINGAPORE · TORONTO

An Archway Paperback
First published in Great Britain
by Simon & Schuster Ltd in 1995
A Paramount Communications Company

Simon & Schuster Ltd
West Garden Place
Kendal Street
London W2 2AQ

AN ARCHWAY PAPERBACK and colophon are registered
trademarks of Simon & Schuster Inc

A CIP catalogue record for this book is
available from the British Library

ISBN 0-671-86515-3

Printed and bound in Great Britain by
HarperCollins*Manufacturing*

For Robert Kiefer and Carol Ponder,
two of the coolest people I know.

CHAPTER
1

Wow. Unbelievable. Awesome. Fantastic. Fabulous. These are words I use a lot.

So sue me, I'm enthusiastic.

The thing I've always been most enthusiastic about is music. Gramma Beth, who is possibly the coolest woman on the face of the earth and an incredible fiddle player, insists that I could sing before I could talk. Sometimes I think my whole life should be orchestrated—you know, like mood music should play in the background during all the most significant moments of my life. I like all kinds of music, so I'm pretty eclectic in my Life Orchestration choices. For example, when I won this talent show last year, I kept hearing the theme song from the old movie *Fame* in my head. When I was thirteen and got kissed for the first time, I really and truly heard "One Hand, One Heart" from *West Side Story* just as this guy's lips pressed against mine.

I think you get the idea.

Another thing I've always been enthusiastic about is my very best friend in the world, Kimmy Carrier. We've been best friends since we were little bitty things. We're complete opposites. Kimmy is tall, blond, thin, Christian, shy, and scared of everything. Well, at least she *used* to be shy and scared of everything. I am short, red-headed like everyone else in my huge family, plump, Jewish, outgoing, and will try just about anything once.

Kimmy and I became best friends on the very first day of kindergarten, when she was crying pitifully out in front of the school, scared to death. I took out my clean white lace hankie—it had been Gramma Beth's when she was a girl, and I thought it was romantic—and handed it to Kimmy. Then I took her hand and led her into the school. Even then I heard music—it was a real "Consider Yourself" kind of moment. That's a song about friendship from that old musical *Oliver!* It's really good, in case you've never seen it.

I was thinking about all this on a Saturday

night, as I got dressed for a gig with my band, Wild Hearts. I had always dreamed of having my own band, and just recently that dream had come true. Kimmy had always been the biggest supporter of my dream, next to Gramma Beth.

You see, one thing Kimmy and I always had in common is music. She is this incredible lead guitar player—I mean, the girl is major-league talented.

Until recently, though, no one knew this but me, because Kimmy Carrier was so shy that she actually would not play in front of anyone but yours truly. I begged her—I mean, literally begged her—to join my band. Well, I got my wish. And now *everyone* knows how talented Kimmy is.

But that's not the only thing that has changed. She's started dressing cooler, standing up straighter, and asserting herself. She even has a boyfriend, a very terrific guy named Sawyer Paxton, whose dad is a famous country songwriter.

Now, I am happy for Kimmy. I really am. The fact that I don't have a boyfriend because guys always treat me like a friend instead of a girlfriend doesn't mean I begrudge Kimmy having a boyfriend. A cool, cute, talented, nice boyfriend. And the fact that Kimmy was finally learning to assert herself and quit being so wimpy made me real happy for her. Real.

Yep, my best friend was asserting herself so much that that very night I would find out if Kimmy was going to assert herself right out of my band.

She wasn't sure she really wanted to be in Wild Hearts. She said she felt like a phony, pretending she was some kind of country rock star. She also felt guilty, because this guy named Dave Mallone, who had a crush on her, had actually gone nutso and shot Sawyer Paxton in the arm over his love for Kimmy. She felt responsible. Now all she wanted was to drop out of the band and spend every moment by Sawyer's side.

Well, I couldn't let that happen. I needed Kimmy. Not only because she is by far the best lead guitarist I could hope to find but also because Kimmy still is and always will be my best friend.

Even if maybe she doesn't need me anymore.

I pulled on my cowboy boots, which looked very cute with my short denim skirt and fringed vest. Then I sprayed a little perfume through my red curls, picked up my purse, and headed downstairs to wait for Sandra to pick me up in her Jeep.

Sandra "don't call me Sandy" Farrell is our bass player. She is African American, very cute, very smart, and the most accomplished person I ever met in my life. I mean, she is president of the junior class, captain of the tennis team, and she plays four—count 'em, four—musical instruments well. She also doesn't take any crap from anyone. She's kind of intimidating to a lot of the kids at school. Like me, sometimes.

Sandra showed up right on time, and Jane McVay, our drummer, was already in the front seat. Jane is one of a kind. She recently moved to Nashville from New York City, where she went to that famous high school, the High School of Performing Arts. She is a seriously kick-ass drummer, and she knows it. She's also really funny—she dresses in costumes that she puts together from places like the Salvation Army—she's sort of like her own art project.

"Hey, ya'll," I called, as I climbed into the back of Sandra's Jeep.

"What's shaking?" Jane asked. Sandra pulled out into the street, and Jane let the wind whip her hair across her face. "Hey, who is the kid who's having this party, again?"

"Lee Fountain," I reported. "He's a senior at Brentwood High. It's his birthday."

Jane turned around to face me. "We're getting bucks for this, right?"

"Right," I confirmed, raising my voice over the wind. "A hundred for the night."

Jane shook her head ruefully. "Oh, great," she groaned. "Twenty-five bucks apiece. At this rate I'll be in debt to my mother for the rest of my life."

Jane had recently had to take a job at Uncle Zap's, a record store in the mall, in order to pay her mom back for damage done to her mother's car. Jane had gone out on a date with Wyatt Shane, one of the true jerks of the Western world, and he'd gotten drunk, driven Jane's mom's car, and wrecked it.

"Speaking of money," Sandra called to us as she made a turn onto Tyne Boulevard, "you guys need to chip in for gas, okay?" Sandra says "you guys" instead of "ya'll" because she's from Detroit. It's a dead Yankee giveaway.

We turned onto the private drive that led to Kimmy's mother's mansion, and I marveled again at just how rich Kimmy's family is. Her parents are divorced, and they have separate mansions in adjacent neighborhoods. They have joint custody of Kimmy, and she goes back and forth between their houses. She's extremely uncomfortable about being so rich, and she tries to hide her wealth from the world.

"This place still weirds me out," Jane murmured as Sandra pulled the Jeep up the circular drive and honked the horn for Kimmy. "Do you think they used to have slaves?"

Sandra laughed. "It isn't a plantation, Jane," she said dryly.

"Whatever," Jane replied darkly. "All I know is if I was black I could never live in the South."

Sandra turned to Jane, an amused look on her face. "Trust me, there's racism everywhere, Jane. You think there isn't racism in New York?"

"Oh, sure," Jane agreed, "everyone hates everyone in New York. But they're very up-front about it."

Kimmy came running out the front door, her guitar case clutched in her hand. "Sorry, ya'll," she said breathlessly, climbing into the back seat next to me. "I was on the phone with Sawyer at the hospital."

Sandra put the car into gear and pulled out of the driveway. "How is he?" she asked Kimmy.

"He's much better," Kimmy replied, a ridiculous grin of love on her face. "He's getting released real soon."

"And you get to nurse him back to health, huh?" Jane asked.

"I want to," Kimmy said solemnly.

I smiled a supportive smile at Kimmy. Of course she wanted to be with Sawyer. If I was in love for the very first time and had a major cool boyfriend who had been shot *over me*, I would definitely want to be by his side.

But of course I didn't, and Kimmy did.

We found Lee's house, a sprawling ranch on Franklin Road, and pulled the Jeep around near the patio in back, which was where Lee had told us to set up. My older twin brothers, Dustin and Dylan—twenty years old, students at Vanderbilt University, and according to my friends, "to-die-for cute"—had brought the heavy equipment over earlier, so all we had to do was sashay in with our instruments and our cute selves.

We did look cute, too. Although we'd gone together to Dangerous Threads and purchased stage outfits, we didn't wear them when we played private parties. Instead, we all wore whatever we felt like wearing, and that was working out great. Sandra had on Daisy Duke cutoff jeans with a white ruffled blouse and flat-heeled black ankle boots. Jane had on black jeans with a flannel shirt and a denim jacket with the sleeves cut off that had a portrait of Jim Morrison on fire hand-painted on it. And Kimmy had on a short red skirt held up by denim suspenders under which she wore a man's white T-shirt. She wore light makeup, and her long blond hair looked fabulous, flowing over her shoulders. It was so strange. When I squinted, I saw the old Kimmy, the one I had known forever, the one who wore baggy, nondescript clothes, who did her best to look plain and blend into the woodwork.

"Hey, Savy," Lee said, coming out on to the patio through the sliding glass doors. There were already maybe three dozen kids milling around, laughing, talking—screaming, actually—above a sound system that was blaring out an old Grateful Dead tape. Kimmy ran inside to use the john while the rest of us made sure everything was set up.

"Hi," I replied with a grin. Lee is short but he has a very cute face. He's seventeen, quiet, kind of shy, the younger brother of Dustin and Dylan's friend, Calvin Fountain, which may have something to do with how we got this gig. Actually, I always thought that Lee was really fine, in a quiet kind of way. He is one of the guys I was referring to who treat me like a "friend" instead of a "girlfriend." Maybe it was just because I'd known Lee since we were both kids tagging after the older guys. But I'd kind of always had this fantasy that one day he would see me as a Girl with a capital *G*.

"Happy birthday!" I cried, giving him a big kiss on the cheek. "You expecting a crowd?" I asked him, checking the vocal mike that was set up at my electric piano.

"Oh, you know, whatever," he said with a shy shrug and a grin. I thought he looked nervous. It's hard to plan a party and not know if it's going to be a success.

9

"Don't worry," I assured him, "your party is going to be a smash. So, can we do a sound check?" I asked him.

"Well, kids are already here, so I don't think that would be cool," Lee said nervously.

"We have to do a sound check," Sandra said flatly, draping the strap of her bass guitar around her neck.

"Uh, but it would, like, break the mood," Lee explained. He moved closer to me. "You know, quiet isn't good at a party."

"So, why do you have people here at the same time as you told us to come set up?" Jane asked Lee over the Grateful Dead.

He shrugged again. "I guess I got my times goofed up. So could you just skip the sound check?"

I glanced at Jane and Sandra. They both looked disgusted, but what could I do? "Okay," I finally said with a sigh.

"Sorry," Kimmy said breathlessly, running out of the house. One bad habit she hasn't broken is that she still apologizes all the time.

"Kimmy?" Lee asked, his jaw hanging open. Lee had hung around our house with his older brother over the years, so he'd known Kimmy for years, too. Since Kimmy hates her own home, she spends most of her time at mine. At least she used to. Lee hadn't yet seen the new Kimmy.

Kimmy smiled shyly. "Hi, Lee," she said.

"You look . . . unbelievable," he finally managed.

Kimmy blushed. "Oh, no, I really don't . . ."

"Yeah, you really do," Lee insisted, yelling over the music. "Wow."

The music ended right before Lee said "Wow," leaving a giant hush out there on the patio.

"Okay, everyone ready?" I asked the band, ignoring the fact that Lee was still standing there staring at the new Kimmy Carrier. We'd figured out our sets at our last band practice, and knew we were going to start with an old Creedence Clearwater Revival tune, "Proud Mary."

Lee actually walked backwards so that he could keep looking at Kimmy, until he stumbled over a rock and turned around. I counted off the first number, and we began to play.

I sang lustily into the vocal mike, running the keyboard riffs I had practiced so long and hard. Kimmy rocked out on the guitar, closing her eyes so she could tune out everyone and everything but the music. Sandra came in rock steady on the bass, and Jane kicked in her hot backbeat.

People started dancing right away—always a good sign—and soon the patio was crowded with kids boogying to the music. We interspersed country and rock tunes with originals that Jane had written. Dang, but we sounded good. I got this rush of happiness as I sang my heart out into that vocal mike. This was only the beginning! Wild Hearts could be so big!

After the first set we took a break, and someone cranked up the Grateful Dead again. Sandra and Jane went inside to cool off in the air conditioning. I went to get a diet Coke from a plastic trash can full of drinks and ice, and I sat down on a nearby bench. Kimmy got a bottle of apple juice and sat down next to me.

"It's going great, huh?" I asked Kimmy.

She nodded and gulped back some of the juice.

"I love that new song Jane wrote," I continued. "I think we should try and demo it."

Kimmy knew that I meant we should make a recording of the song so that we could peddle it to famous artists who might decide to record it, or so that some producer or record label might hear it and take an interest in our band.

Kimmy looked doubtful. "I don't know, it's kind of soon for that."

"No time like the present," I insisted, watching a couple kissing passionately on the other side of the huge patio. "That is so lame," I commented.

Kimmy looked over at the couple. "I think it's romantic," she said dreamily.

I gave her a look. "Swapping spit in public like that? Are you nuts?"

"Well, maybe they just really love each other and can't help themselves," she suggested. "It happens."

Through the sliding glass doors I saw Lee talking to a cute Asian girl with gorgeous long hair. He caught my eye and gave me a nice wave, then started out toward the patio. A slow tune came on, and a bunch of couples started to dance. Lee came right over to me. Yes! He was going to ask me to slow-dance!

"Hey, y'all sounded great," he told me eagerly.

"Thanks," I said, grinning widely.

He turned to Kimmy. "Would you like to dance?"

Kimmy looked surprised. "Me? Oh, oh, no, I—"

"Come on," Lee coaxed. "It'll be fun." He took Kimmy's hand, and she got up with him, then went into his arms.

I smiled at Kimmy, but in my evil heart of hearts I was happy to see that she was taller than he was and they looked stupid together.

Lee obviously couldn't have cared less. He just grinned up into her sweet face and got that dumb look on his face that guys get when the lust puppy hits them.

It was a real "Out of My Shoes Tonight" by

Lorrie Morgan kind of moment, where Lorrie sings about wanting to be this other girl because this other girl is the one the guy she likes really wants.

Yeah, but what does Lorrie know? *She* probably never had a guy think of *her* as just a friend.

CHAPTER 2

♡

*T*hose people are getting up. Snag the booth!"
I cried to Jane, who was the first one into the
crowded restaurant. After we'd finished playing
at Lee's party, we headed over to Musical Burgers near Vanderbilt, our favorite hang. It's open
twenty-four hours, so a lot of studio musicians go
there after their recording sessions, which last
until all hours. They also have great cheap food
and a kickin' jukebox.

The four of us slid into the back booth, Kimmy
next to me, Jane and Sandra on the other side.
Garth Brooks's latest hit was booming out of the
jukebox, and there I was with my band, after a
job where I actually got paid to sing. I'm not a

person who hangs on to a mad for long, so I felt really happy.

"Ya'll aren't going to believe this," Kimmy said, settling back into the booth, "but Lee Fountain asked me out!"

A little of my happiness slid away. But that was silly. I should have been happy for Kimmy! "Cool beans!" I told her, giving her a grin. "You going?"

"Of course not!" she protested. "I could never! I love Sawyer!"

Keep in mind that Kimmy had never had an actual *date* until Sawyer asked her out.

"So, did you and Sawyer decide you weren't going to date anyone else?" Sandra asked Kimmy.

"Well, no," she admitted. "I mean, we haven't actually talked about it."

" 'Too many fish in the sea!' " Jane sang out a line from a really old rock song. " 'Short ones, tall ones, big ones, small ones—' "

"I'm in love," Kimmy said gravely. "I don't care about the other fish."

"Hi, I'm Bettina, and I'll be your waitress tonight," a pale girl with long, bedraggled hair coming lose from its clip said, striving for "perky" and failing miserably.

We all gave Bettina a funny look. Musical

Burgers is a very laid-back kind of place. The staff is definitely not perky.

"Are you new here?" I asked her cautiously.

"Yeah, it's my first day," she confided. "I was waitressing at the Family Fun Pizza House before this."

That explained it. The waitresses at the Family Fun Pizza House were so enthusiastic they made me look depressed. They were trained to act that way. They even said "God bless!" when they gave you the Family Fun Check after your meal. My little brother, Timmy, likes to go there and play the video games.

"You don't need to be Miss Congeniality here," Sandra told Bettina with a smile. "The kids and the musicians who come in here will run you ragged."

"I guess," Bettina replied with a sigh, "but old habits die hard. I wasn't perky enough for the Family Fun Pizza House, so I got fired. I'm a singer, see, and I've got this independent deal on the Houseafire label, but I haven't actually made any money yet. So I really need this job."

"Excuse me, waitress, we're still waitin' on those burgers!" a guy called from the next table.

"Oh, rats, I forgot their burgers. They wanted them rare, and now they'll be well done from sitting under the warmer," Bettina muttered anxiously. She turned back to us. "Can I take your order?"

We quickly ordered burgers all around, except for Jane, who had decided recently that eating animals was disgusting. She ordered a grilled cheese sandwich. We all ordered the special homemade lemonade.

"Hey, waitress, our burgers?" the guy at the next table called again, sounding ticked off. Bettina hurried away.

"See, things could be worse," I told Jane. "You could be working here instead of at Uncle Zap's."

"Uncle Zap's is worse," Jane insisted. "At least a waitress gets to move around. I'm stuck on that stool behind the cash register like some kind of lump."

"So how long is it going to take you to earn enough to pay your mom back?" Kimmy wondered.

Jane snorted. "Forever. I'm not kidding. We're talking indentured servitude. Speaking of which, I got my schedule for next week. I have to work every single night."

"So when are we supposed to have band practice?" I asked her.

Jane shrugged. "Got me. How about if I don't sleep?"

"But we're supposed to be getting ready for that Battle of the Bands at Vanderbilt!" I cried. "We've got to practice!"

"I can't practice next week, either," Sandra said. "I've got student council stuff Monday and Tuesday, and tennis stuff the rest of the week."

"Two Cokes, two diet Cokes," Bettina said, putting the drinks on the table.

"Sorry, but we ordered lemonade," Sandra told her.

"Miss! These burgers are well done!" the guy at the next table called.

"Oh, God," Bettina said, putting her head in her hands. "I'm sorry, I'm really sorry," she told us, picking up the Cokes and scurrying off.

"Listen, ya'll, we have to practice at least one day next week," I told my friends in an even voice. "We have to find a way."

Kimmy looked at her watch. "Can you excuse me a minute? I just want to call Sawyer at the hospital and say good night before he falls asleep."

I stood up to let Kimmy out of the booth. Then I sat back down. My bad mood, which had turned into a good mood, was quickly turning into an awful mood.

"Look, maybe we could set up a certain night as a regular time to rehearse during the week, and then we could make up the other time on the weekends," I tried.

"Next weekend my family is going camping," Jane said, rolling her eyes.

"But you can't!" I protested.

"Yeah? Tell my parents that," Jane replied, flipping through the tunes on the jukebox. "We held a family meeting and voted on it. I voted no, and my little sister, Jill-the-suck-up, voted yes with my parents, per usual."

"I've got a tennis tournament out of town next weekend, anyway," Sandra said.

"Lemonade, right?" Bettina asked, holding four glasses in her hands. "Please tell me it was lemonade."

"You're right," I assured her, and she set the glasses down gratefully.

"Oh, I love this tune—'He's a Rebel,' " Jane said, coming upon the oldie in the jukebox listings. "We should cover that!"

Bettina's eyes lit up. "Are ya'll a band?"

"Yeah, Wild Hearts," I said proudly.

"Do you need a singer?" she asked us hopefully.

"Sorry," I said. "I sing lead."

"Oh, well, that's okay," she said, sounding disappointed. She hurried off.

"Of course we're not going to be much of a

band, if we don't rehearse," I added pointedly to Jane and Sandra.

Kimmy came rushing back to the table. "Sawyer says hey," she told us, sliding into the booth. "He says he can go home in a day or two!"

"That's great!" I told Kimmy, and I really meant it. When Sawyer got shot in front of all of us, it was the worst thing I'd ever seen in my life. All that blood. We didn't know if he'd even live.

"Isn't he the greatest?" Kimmy asked us dreamily.

"We were just planning a regular weeknight for band practice," I told Kimmy, trying to help her get with the program.

"Oh, well, I have to wait and see how things are with Sawyer," she explained earnestly.

"Kimmy, don't plan your life around a guy," Sandra suggested, sipping her lemonade.

"But he's what I care about!" Kimmy said. She turned to me. "Look, I told you I wanted you to replace me in the band—"

"I don't want to talk about that now," I said quickly.

"Well, I haven't changed my mind," Kimmy insisted. "I just wanted you to know."

Great. Just great. Jane and Sandra were too busy for the band, and my best friend still wanted to quit.

Even my enthusiastic nature couldn't stand up against all that. I fell silent, feeling beaten, and soon Bettina came back with our food. "I hope I got it right," she said, putting the food on the table. And here," she added, slipping a demo tape out of her pocket. "Just in case you ever do need a singer. I carry my tape with me everywhere!"

"Thanks," Sandra said politely, and started to put the tape in her purse.

"I'll take it," Kimmy said, reaching for the tape. "I'll give it to Sawyer. He's always looking for singers to demo his stuff."

I looked at Kimmy. I thought *we* were going to demo Sawyer's stuff when he didn't want to sing the song himself for some reason. How could Kimmy do that to me?

But she didn't even notice how I felt. She just reached for her burger and took a big bite. Even that was new. Kimmy was famous for eating like a bird.

Everything was changing. And not necessarily for the better.

"Hi, how did it go?" Dustin asked me when I walked into the house later that night. He was sitting in the music room writing song lyrics. He's a music composition major at Vanderbilt, and his identical twin, Dylan, is a music ed major. They are both six feet tall, with auburn hair, big brown eyes, and matching dimples in their chins.

"Okay," I said listlessly, falling onto the couch next to him. I had to move a roll of wallpaper out of the way. Our house is always in a state of redecoration hell. It's supposed to be an ongoing family project.

"That doesn't sound too good," Dustin said, putting his pencil down.

I shrugged and put my boot-clad feet up on the coffee table. "We're having a hard time finding a night when everyone can rehearse," I told him.

"Yeah, bands always run into that little snag," he commiserated.

"Well, I don't see why!" I cried. "I mean, not if everyone is committed!"

"So who isn't committed?"

I shrugged morosely. "Jane has this stupid part-time job, and Sandra is Miss Everything at school, and Kimmy is so in love with this guy that she acts like she's had a lobotomy!"

"Tough, huh?"

"Maybe I should just write songs, like you," I groused. "Then I wouldn't have to depend on anybody else."

"Hey, sweetie, I thought I heard your voice." It was Gramma Beth, wrapped up in her favorite ancient Chinese robe that she actually got in China. She went there years ago, right after my grandfather died. She said she'd always wanted to see China, and so she went. Alone. And thought nothing of it.

"How was the gig?" she asked me.

I shrugged.

"Savy's having band problems," Dustin explained.

"Nu?" she asked. "Want to tell me over some food?" Gramma Beth has an interesting combination of a Jewish grandmother's sensibilities with a no-holds-barred southern flavor sprinkled with a little Yiddish. *Nu,* for example, means "So?" "I made a pound cake, and there's fresh strawberries to go on top."

I shook my head no. "We ate at Musical Burgers."

Gramma Beth made a face. "That is not what I call food."

I had to laugh. My grandmother is convinced that I will get poisoned from eating in bad restaurants.

"So, tell me what's up," she encouraged me, helping me to pull off my cowboy boots. She put my feet in her lap and began to rub them. It was heaven.

So I told her all about the problems I was having with the band, and how everyone was too busy to rehearse.

"They're putting everything else before the music," I said. "Which means we'll never be more than second rate!"

My grandmother nodded thoughtfully. "You're right, my girl. No commitment always equals no excellence. Things have got to change."

"Well, I don't know how," I replied.

"Maybe it's just this week," she said. "You need to give this a bit of time. You could use this week to catch up on your studies, things like that."

I looked closely at my grandmother. She never says things like "catch up on your studies." She thinks people learn more from life than they do from school.

Unfortunately my parents don't agree with her.

"Who've you been talking to, Mom or Dad?" I asked her, putting my feet down on the rug.

"Both," she admitted. "They think you're not studying enough."

"What else is new?" I asked. I looked over at my brother. "I can't wait until I'm in college, like you."

Dustin laughed. "Hey, Mom and Dad still rag on me to study."

"Yeah, but you don't have to listen," I pointed out. "And you don't have to take stupid classes that you have no interest in. Someone tell me, please, how knowing geometry is going to change my life!"

"I have no idea," my grandmother said honestly. She got up from the couch. "Well, if I can't interest anyone in food, I'm off to bed." She leaned down to kiss me. "Sweet dreams, little one."

I lay down on the couch and put the pillow over my head. "All I want is to have a great band! Why is that so tough?"

Dustin took the pillow off my head. "Hey, I've got an idea."

"What?"

"You want to come to this party with me tomorrow night?"

I sat up. "What party?" Dustin and Dylan never invite me to their parties.

"It's at a frat house at Vanderbilt," Dustin explained. "This guy I know manages the band that's playing, Jack Flash. I heard 'em at a party last semester, and they are major-league hot."

"A college party? College guys?" I asked.

"Yeah, and they're all too old for you, so don't get any ideas," my brother said. "But I'll introduce you to Trey, and you can ask him how he gets the band to make a commitment, stuff like that. Okay?"

"You're the greatest!" I told him, hugging him exuberantly.

"Thanks," Dustin said. "Just remember, college guys are too old for you."

Ha.

CHAPTER
3

It took me forever to decide what to wear the next night. I wanted to look great, but I didn't want to look like I was trying too hard. I finally decided on my favorite worn jeans and a big flannel shirt, but I wore a camisole under the flannel shirt and left a button unbuttoned so that the camisole would show. I put on a little makeup—masacara, eyeliner—sprayed myself with perfume, and I was ready.

"You're wearing that to a party?" my mom asked when I walked into the family room where she, my father, my little brother, Timmy, and my little sister, Shelly, were watching a video they'd rented. My mom put the video on pause.

"What?" I asked, looking down at myself.

"I think you look cute," my sister offered.

I smiled at her. Shelly's eleven and very sweet. I actually like all three of my brothers and my sister, which I guess is unusual.

"Savy honey, is your homework all done for tomorrow?" my dad asked me.

"Oh, sure," I said, but I squirmed a little. I hate to lie to my parents, but let's face it, sometimes it's a necessity.

"Don't stay out past eleven, please," my mom said. "Tomorrow is school. Get one of your brothers to drive you home, even if they're going back out."

"I'll drive her," Dustin offered, ambling into the room eating an apple. "Dylan is out somewhere. I don't think he's going to this party. You ready?" he asked me.

"Yeah," I replied. I kissed my parents goodbye, and Dustin and I headed out the door.

"Did I dress okay?" I asked my brother in the car.

He looked over at me. "Yeah, I guess," he said.

I sighed. I was just his little sister. He had no sense of me as a Girl. Neither did any of his friends. Just once I'd like to have one of his friends flirt with me or ask me out or—this was my ultimate fantasy—kiss me passionately.

Please don't think that I haven't had dates, because that wouldn't be true. I've had lots of dates with lots of guys. Fun dates. Group dates with a lot of kids. I've even been kissed by some cute guys that I liked. But somehow it had never blossomed into the Big Romance. Like what Kimmy found the first time out.

The party was loud and wild already when we arrived. There was a keg of beer in the corner of the living room, and everyone seemed to be downing it rapidly. I can't stand beer myself, and personally I hate the way most people act when they've been drinking. But most kids drink—that's just the reality.

I poured myself a Coke from the bottle on the table. The ice had all melted into a pool of water so I was forced to drink it warm. I looked around for my brother, but he was talking with some very cute girl, so I figured I should leave him alone.

From in the next room I heard great music and a hot singer wailing away. I made my way through the crowd until I could see the band. The lead singer was a very thin girl with long, straight blond hair parted in the middle. She had on a very short antique-looking lace dress, the kind you'd find in a used-clothing store. Her hands were wrapped around the mike, her eyes were

closed, and she was singing in a sexy, low-pitched
growl that made the hairs on the back of my neck
stand up. I mean, she was, really, really good.
Behind her, the band was cooking. I stood there
listening through the rest of the band's set, about
four songs, and as soon as they took a break I
went right over to the girl who had been singing.

"Hi!" I said, putting out my hand. "I'm Savy
Leeman. Listen, I have to tell you how great
you are!"

The girl took my hand in her tiny, slim fingers.
"Hi, Savy, I'm Krissy. Krissy McCaine."

"You are so fabulous!" I bubbled enthusiasti-
cally. "I just love your voice!"

"Thanks again," Krissy said. She wiped at her
damp forehead with a Kleenex.

"I'm a singer, too," I told her eagerly. "I have
this all-girl band called Wild Hearts."

"Yeah?" Krissy asked.

I nodded. "We're more country than your
band, and we're not as far along, but—"

"Hey, I need to get a drink," Krissy interrupted. "You want to come?"

"Sure," I replied. "There's beer or warm
Coke."

Krissy smiled. "Come with me." She picked up
her purse and led me upstairs to a bathroom,
which we entered. Then she locked the door and

sat on the edge of the tub. "I brought my own." She opened her purse and pulled out a pint of scotch, then took a long swallow. "Ooo, much better," she sighed in her gravelly voice. "You want?" She held the bottle out to me.

"No, thanks," I said, leaning against the door. "So, how long has your band been together?" I asked her.

"A little over a year," she told me, swallowing some more scotch. "We're doing a showcase for some labels next month. Trey—he's our manager—thinks we have a good shot at getting a deal."

I knew what she meant. A showcase meant that the band would play at one of the big clubs in town, and all the executives from the various record labels would be invited. If someone was impressed enough with the band, they'd get offered a recording contract or at least a development deal, and they'd be on their way.

"God, I just dream of being far enough along to do a major showcase," I said with a sigh. "I know we're good enough—or at least we could be. But it's so hard to get everyone to commit!"

"Well, Trey handles that," Krissy said. "If someone isn't committed, they're out. He put us on a regular rehearsal schedule, he got us into the studio, he decided on our sound, our look, the whole deal."

"So how did you find Trey?" I asked eagerly.

"He found me," Krissy said with a grin. "I was singing in this dive, and he found me and put Jack Flash together. He's just unbelievable as a manager." She gulped back another swallow of scotch. "Sometimes he's a pain in the ass, but, hey, you can't have everything, can you?"

There was a knock on the door.

"Krissy?" came a masculine voice. "You in there?"

Krissy shook her head violently and pointed at me, indicating I should speak.

"Uh, I'm in here!" I called out.

"Oh, sorry," the voice said.

Krissy held up her hand to me, as if she was making sure the person was out of earshot. "That was Trey, checking up on me. You see what I mean about his being a pain in the ass."

"Why does he check up on you?"

She laughed. "He thinks I shouldn't drink." She reached into her purse, took out a small vial of pills, and popped one into her mouth. "You want? It's an upper."

"No, thanks," I said. "Uh, maybe you shouldn't mix that with the scotch."

"Please," she scoffed. "Believe me, I know exactly what I can handle." She stood up and slung her purse over her shoulder. "Come on, let's go take a walk before Trey finds me."

We were just walking out the front door when Krissy's bass player stopped her. "Hey, Krissy, Trey is looking for you," he told her.

"No kidding," Krissy said sarcastically. "Oh, this is—what was your name again?" she asked me, her voice a little fuzzy around the edges.

"Savy Leeman."

"Savy, this is my bass player, Ryan Black," Krissy said.

Ryan grinned at me and put out his hand for me to shake. He was tall, very skinny, with long brown hair and a sweet smile. "Savy—cool name," he said.

"Thanks. Hey, your band is really good!" I told him.

"We try," he said with a grin. "You a musician?"

"Vocals and keyboards," I replied.

"Oh, yeah? You playing anywhere?" Ryan asked me.

I shook my head. "We're planning to do that big Battle of the Bands, though."

"Hey, we're gonna be in it, too!" Ryan said. "Cool, I'll get to hear you sing."

"There you are," a tall guy said, hurrying over to us. I couldn't help but notice how gorgeous he was. He looked like a movie star. His hair was black and his eyes were a piercing blue. He took

Krissy's arm and leaned close to her to smell her breath. "Krissy . . ." he said in a low, cold voice.

"Oh, chill out, mother," Krissy said crossly. "So I had one little drink." She cocked her head in my direction. "This is my new friend, Savy . . . something-or-other."

"Savy Leeman," I said.

"Savy . . . Oh, you must be Dustin's sister. He just told me you were here," the guy said. "I'm Trey Jackson. We're doing a tune that your brother wrote in the next set."

"Really?" I asked, thrilled. "He didn't tell me you were covering a song he wrote!"

"He's modest," Trey said with a smile. He turned back to Krissy and grabbed her arm again. "Come on. I'm getting you some coffee before the next set." He steered her toward the kitchen.

"He really looks out for ya'll, huh?" I said to Ryan.

"Something like that," Ryan said enigmatically.

I watched Trey as he and Krissy made their way across the room. "If my band had someone like him looking out for us, we could accomplish anything," I said passionately.

"Maybe," Ryan said. "Want to dance?"

"No, thanks," I said absentmindedly. "Maybe I'll just go see if Trey and Krissy need any help."

"They need a lot of help," Ryan said, "but I don't think you're gonna be able to give it to 'em."

I really didn't pay any attention to what Ryan had said, I just said a friendly good-bye and took off for the kitchen.

The beginnings of a plan were forming in my little mind. Maybe, just maybe, Trey could manage two bands at the same time—Jack Flash and Wild Hearts. Why not? We were completely different; they were heavy metal and we were country rock. Trey could be the answer to all my problems with the band. I was completely convinced that everything would change with the band if we had a real professional manager.

Now all I had to do was convince Trey Jackson.

"Hi, come on in," Krissy said, ushering me into the dark hallway of her small frame house in east Nashville.

It was two days later, and when I'd called Krissy the day before, she'd invited me over to hang out. We had exchanged phone numbers at the party Sunday night. Of course she had been so out of it, I wasn't sure she'd even remember me when I called her. In fact, even though she'd invited me over, I still wasn't sure she remembered too much about me. But she did say that she had some demo tapes of the band I could hear, and she also mentioned that Trey would be stopping over.

I hadn't been able to talk with him at the party—he was always with other people, or else he was listening so intently to the band that I couldn't interrupt. Maybe this would be my chance to talk with him about my band.

Before I left the house, my mom asked me if I'd finished my homework. I lied again and said yes, but I vowed to myself that I'd get home early enough to finish the reading I had to do for the quiz that was coming up in my history class.

"So, you want a beer?" Krissy asked me. She looked and acted much more together than she had either at the party or on the phone. She had on clean jeans and a gauzy shirt, and her hair looked freshly washed.

"No, thanks," I said, and followed her into the tiny living room. An old upright piano stood in the corner with sheet music strewn over the top of it. Other than that, there was one dilapidated print couch and an upholstered chair with the stuffing coming out on the sides.

"Do you live alone?" I asked Krissy, skirting a large cobweb in the corner.

"No, the drummer from Jack Flash lives

here—his name is Carl—and his girlfriend, Tanya. I just moved in a couple of weeks ago, actually." She went to the fridge, got herself a diet Coke, and handed me one, too.

"So, where did you live before?" I asked curiously, taking a seat in the stuffed chair.

"With Trey," Krissy said, plopping herself down on the couch. "He's got a great apartment in this complex out in Bellevue—swimming pool, all that." She took a large gulp of Coke. "But you know how it is, when a couple lives together and works together, it can get too intense. And Lord knows Trey is intense enough without my living with him!"

"Oh, sure," I agreed casually, even though I hadn't actually realized that Krissy and Trey were an item.

"So you wanted to hear one of our demos, right?" Krissy asked me.

"Yeah, I'd love to."

She got up and rummaged through some tapes in a box in the corner of the room, and when she found the one she wanted she stuck it into the tape player that sat on the floor next to the box.

"Your brother wrote this song," Krissy told me. The mournful sounds of Krissy singing a smoky ballad filled the room.

It's a hurtin' kind of love
When we touch but cannot stay.
It's a hurtin' kind of love
When you always turn away.
After I whisper your name in the night,
Cuz that's a hurtin' kind of love, baby.
Don't be a hurtin' love tonight.

Krissy's voice soared and leaped. It filled my heart with the magic of the tormented lyrics that my brother had written. *My brother!* I was so proud.

"That is just unbelievably great," I told Krissy when the tune ended. "I mean, wow, I don't even know what to say—"

"I guess that means you liked it," she said with a grin.

"Liked it? I loved it! How'd you get that kind of vocal control?" I demanded. "How'd you get that sound?"

"I've got this great voice teacher that Trey found for me," Krissy said. "Her name is Sarah Carlton. She's from North Carolina by way of New York. She's really amazing."

"God, I'd love to be able to do that with my voice," I said wistfully.

"I'll give you her phone number," Krissy offered,

looking around for some paper. "She's expensive, but worth it."

"I can't afford to study with anyone," I said glumly, sitting back in the chair. "Anyway, my parents think it would kill my natural style. They're self-taught musicians—they don't believe in lessons."

"So, let's hear what your style is," Krissy suggested, finishing off her Coke.

"What?" I asked, caught off guard.

"I mean let's hear you sing," Krissy said, reaching out to pull me up.

Just then the doorbell rang, and Krissy dropped my hand and ran to the door. "Hi, baby," she said. I peeked out after her. It was Trey. He looked amazingly hot in jeans and a blue T-shirt that matched the blue of his eyes.

He was hugging Krissy, but he saw me over her shoulder. "Hi. You look familiar," he said, eyeing me curiously.

"I'm Dustin Leeman's sister, Savy," I reminded him. "We met at that party Sunday night."

"Oh, sure," he said. He picked up a brown paper bag that he'd brought in with him and handed it to Krissy. "Healthy food," he told her. "Be sure you eat it."

She pecked him on the cheek and carried the food into the kitchen. "You take such good care of me," she told him. "Hey, Savy was just about to sing for me," she called from the kitchen.

"Oh, yeah?" Trey asked with interest, sitting on the couch.

Yes, this could be my big chance!

"Well, if ya'll are sure you really want to hear me," I demurred, not wanting to appear too eager.

"Sure, give it a go," Trey said. "Your brother told me you're really good."

"He did?" I said with wonder. Huh. You can't usually count on your older brother to go around braggin' on you.

"He did," Trey assured me. Krissy went and sat with him, snuggling close.

I sat down at the piano and gave it a few riffs, to check out the touch and the tune. It was an old piano, but it was in really good shape.

"You want to hear country or what?" I asked them.

"You pick," Krissy said easily.

Country, I figured. I couldn't compete with Krissy in the growly voice department, but I bet she couldn't sing country, either. So I closed my eyes and sang that old Linda Ronstadt song, "Faithless Love." It's on her old *Heart Like a Wheel* album, and it is a wondrous thing.

I played the final haunting chords and opened my eyes.

"Let me tell you something," Trey said, his eyes shining. "Your brother didn't lie. You can really sing!"

"I loved it, too," Krissy agreed.

"Really?" I asked, completely thrilled.

"Really," Trey insisted. "And I'm a tough critic."

I spun around on the piano bench. "Well, you know, I have this band—"

Trey wasn't listening. He was looking at Krissy. "Have you eaten anything today?" he asked her.

She sighed. "I don't remember."

"Go eat," he instructed her.

"I'm not hungry," she said petulantly.

"Go eat," he said in a steely voice. "Please," he added.

Krissy kissed Trey on the forehead and got up. "We aim to please!" she called out to him and headed for the kitchen.

He grinned at me. "I have to watch out for her," he explained.

"She's lucky to have you," I said fervently. "Listen, I wanted to tell you about my band. We're called Wild Hearts, and we're an all-girl band, and—"

"All girls because you look cute or all girls who can play?" Trey questioned.

"Both," I said audaciously. I learned that from

Gramma Beth. Nothing ventured, nothing gained, I always say. "So, I was wondering if you'd listen to us play sometime."

"You got a gig coming up soon?" Trey asked me.

"No," I admitted, my hopes falling. "But you could come to band practice!" I added.

Trey shook his head no. "I hate band practice. It's not the same. I would be willing to listen to a demo, though, if you've got one."

"Oh, we do!" I assured him, even though we really didn't. But I knew we could make one, and quickly, too.

"So mail it to me," Trey said, handing me a business card. "I'll listen to it. But I'm warning you, I'm going to tell you the truth, no matter what I think. So if you don't want to hear the truth, don't send it to me."

"I absolutely want to hear the truth," I insisted. "My band is the most important thing in the world to me."

He gave me a new, appraising look. "Yeah?" he asked.

"Yes," I said firmly. "I will do whatever it takes to make it."

"Does everybody in your band feel the same way?" Trey asked me.

"Yes," I lied.

"Let me hear you sing again," he asked, crossing

his legs and sitting back on the couch. "Something up-tempo, maybe?"

I sat back down at the piano and did "Blue Suede Shoes." Then I did "It Wasn't God Who Made Honky Tonk Angels," and then I did one of Jane's originals called "I'd Do Anything."

Trey was sitting a little farther forward with each song that I sang, looking a little bit more interested.

I hardly noticed Krissy standing at the door to the living room, the look on her face getting colder and colder and colder.

CHAPTER 4

$\heartsuit$

That wasn't too hard, huh?" Kimmy said as we walked out of American history class together the next day.

Ms. Millman had given us a quiz about the Boston Tea Party, which I was sure I had flunked royally.

Maybe the fact that I hadn't even read the assigned chapters in our history book had something to do with it.

I'd meant to read them, really meant to. But somehow I'd been so excited about the possibility of Trey Jackson managing Wild Hearts that I hadn't gotten home until eleven, just squeaking in at my curfew. And then . . . well, and then I forgot.

"It wasn't a big quiz," I said, as we turned the corner toward the cafeteria. "I mean, it wasn't like it was a major test or anything."

Kimmy looked at me. "What, did you flunk it?"

I nodded morosely.

"I would have studied with you last night," she said.

"I was busy last night," I explained, "with something more important than that dumb quiz."

I expected Kimmy to ask me right away what I'd been busy with, but she didn't. Instead she said, "I can't believe Sawyer is finally getting out of the hospital today! What do you think I should wear when I go over to his house tonight?"

"How about Saran Wrap?" I suggested. "It's subtle and yet mysterious."

Kimmy stopped walking and pushed a lock of her hair behind her ear. She was wearing one of her old baggy skirts, but with it she had on a man's vest we'd found on one of Jane's excursions to a secondhand store. Her glasses were stashed in her purse, and she had on a little makeup. Her hair was loose and perfect-looking. She looked extremely cute. "Are you mad at me?" she asked in a soft, quavery voice.

"No, of course not!" I insisted.

"Are you sure?"

"Sure I'm sure!"

"Hey, Kimmy, what's under that vest, babe?" Wyatt Shane called to Kimmy as he strode down the hall in the other direction with two of his friends. "Want to play hide-and-seek?"

Kimmy blushed furiously, and I gave Wyatt the evil eye. This guy is a plague on all humanity, as far as I'm concerned. So what if he is incredibly hot-looking? He had made both Jane and Kimmy miserable in the past, and I had no reason to believe he wouldn't continue to spread his misery around in the future.

"Do I look awful?" Kimmy asked in a whisper, fiddling with the vest.

"No, you look great. Just ignore him," I advised.

"So I don't look . . . slutty?" she whispered this last word in horror. Ever since Kimmy started dressing better and wearing cosmetics, her mother has been telling her she looks and acts slutty. That is so far from the truth as to be comical—except that I guess it's never comical if your own mother says something like that to you.

"Kimmy, you are practically a nun, and you could never look slutty," I insisted.

We went into the cafeteria and sat down at our usual table. Sandra and Jane weren't there yet. I unpacked my lunch—Gramma Beth insists on packing it every day—while Kimmy got in the food line. A few minutes later she carried her tray over to our table and set her tuna salad down.

"So, where were you last night?" she asked me.

I bit into the huge roast chicken sandwich Gramma Beth had made for me. "I was with someone who could change our lives," I said dramatically.

"Well, I hope this mystery person has a spaceship to beam me off this planet," Jane said, overhearing us. She came up next to me and slid into a chair. "I have decided once and for all that Earth truly sucks. Do you know there are kids in the hall circulating a petition to ban books from this school?"

"That's terrible!" Kimmy cried.

"Tell me about it," Jane agreed. "They're wearing these little buttons that say 'Teens for Righteousness'—whatever the hell that means. And my dear friend Katie Lynn Kilroy, Mistress of the Pastel People, is the head of it."

Katie Lynn Kilroy is a hateful girl who makes fun of Jane all the time. Just to be nasty, she started a terrible rumor that Jane had had sex with all these different guys. Katie Lynn and her judgmental, idiotic friends pretend to be good

Christians, but they actually can't tolerate anyone who is different from them in any way. They also wear little pastel outfits most of the time, so Jane dubbed them the Pastel People.

"I am ticked off, so stay out of my way," Sandra warned as she marched over to us. She slammed her books down on the table. "Did you see that nonsense in the hall, those Neanderthals petitioning to ban books? I'm taking this up at the student council meeting, I really am." Sandra kept mumbling to herself as she went off to the food line. Jane followed her.

When they both came back with their food, Sandra was still going on about the book-banning petition, but I was determined to divert her attention.

"Listen, I'd like to discuss some band business," I said, swallowing the last of my sandwich. "Some really exciting band business."

"I can't think about the band now!" Sandra cried. She leaned against the table. "Did you ever read *One Flew Over the Cuckoo's Nest*?"

"Of course I read *One Flew Over the Cuckoo's Nest*," I replied.

"Well, they're out there trying to ban *One Flew Over the Cuckoo's Nest*. Also *The Catcher in the Rye*, *Catch-22*, and *To Kill a Mockingbird*."

"Well, they have no brains," I said. "No one

is going to listen to them. What I wanted to tell ya'll is—"

"You don't think anyone is going to listen to them, huh?" Sandra interrupted. "Do you know there are many public schools in this country where idiots like Katie Lynn have actually succeeded in having books banned? We have to make a stand!"

"Look, I agree with you, I just want to tell you about some band stuff! That doesn't make me un-American!"

Sandra looked at me closely. "You're right," she finally said. "But frankly, I'm surprised at you, Savy. This is the kind of thing you usually go wild over."

I took a deep breath. "I will go wild after I tell you my news, okay?"

She dipped her fork into her salad. "I'm listening," she said.

"Speak to me," Jane added hoarsely, imitating Marlon Brando in *The Godfather.*

So I told them about Jack Flash and Trey Jackson, and how he wanted to hear a demo tape of the band. "And I mean this could be a huge break for us!" I finished breathlessly, excited all over again.

"Could be cool," Jane said slowly, licking the spoon from her yogurt, "unless he's gonna try to dictate artistic stuff to us."

"He wouldn't," I swore, even though I really didn't know whether he would or not.

"So what's in it for him?" Sandra asked in her usual pragmatic fashion.

"What's in it for him is big success!" I exclaimed. "Look, managers take a percentage of what the act makes, right?"

Sandra nodded. "When we still lived in Detroit my mom had a manager."

Sandra's mom is a session and demo singer. They moved here from Detroit because there was more work for her in Nashville than there was back home.

"And?" Jane prompted her.

"And he got fifteen percent of everything she made," Sandra said.

"Oh, terrif," Jane grunted. "We make a hundred for the night, and he gets fifteen dollars. That makes so much sense."

"Well, maybe he works out a deal with us for before we start making big bucks," I said evenly. "Which is the whole point."

"The whole point is to have some artistic integrity as a band," Jane reminded me.

"I know that!" I practically yelled, getting more and more frustrated. I lowered my voice. "All I'm saying is that a professional manager can help us become successful. So what do you say?"

"Maybe Sawyer would let us make a demo in his studio," Kimmy suggested in her shy voice.

I grinned. Yes! Something positive about the band from Kimmy! "You think?" I asked. "That would be awesome!"

"I'll ask him tonight," Kimmy promised, returning my smile.

Sandra and Jane went back to talking about the idiotic Teens for Righteousness, but that was okay. Because we were going to make a demo. And Trey was going to decide we were so good that he would manage us and make us a huge success. And then Kimmy couldn't possibly leave the band.

She just couldn't.

"I think that's it!" I said with excitement.

It was the next night, and we were all at the recording studio behind Sawyer's house, where we'd just finished doing demo tapes of two of our tunes. We'd picked our rock arrangement of "It Wasn't God Who Made Honky Tonk Angels" and an original by Jane called "Do Me Right."

Sawyer was sitting on the couch. His arm was still in a sling, but basically he looked hale and healthy again. He kept his eyes on Kimmy most of the time, and she kept her eyes on him—it was a wonder she could find the chords on her guitar. She was wearing jeans and a flannel shirt, but she didn't have on her glasses, and mascara made her huge blue eyes look even huger.

"You sure the harmonies on the bridge on 'Do Me Right' are okay?" Jane asked with a frown.

I nodded. "Even that tricky part where you go to the F-sharp. Let's play it back."

We all listened intently to the mix on the playback. It sounded good. Really good. "So, that's it," I said, taking the tape out of the cassette player. "I know Trey is gonna love this. I am so psyched!"

"Why do ya'll think you need a manager?" Sawyer asked us, pushing some hair out of his eyes with the hand that wasn't in the sling.

"Well, he can get us gigs," I said.

"An agent does that," Sawyer said. "An agent's job is to get you work, and a manager's job is to, like, mold your career."

"Okay, so he can mold our career," I replied.

"Well, like, mold it how?" Kimmy asked skeptically.

A dagger of anger shot through me. She was only talking that way so she'd be agreeing with her beloved boyfriend.

"Like help us get serious about this," I snapped. "Like with our sound and our look and . . . just everything."

"But ya'll are so new at this," Sawyer said. "Not that you aren't great, because you are. But maybe ya'll need to be further along before you think about a manager."

Kimmy listened intently and nodded solemnly. "Uh-huh," she agreed.

"But that's the whole point," I explained patiently. "A manager can help us get further along."

"Not unless he's serious and is hooked in to your musical style," Jane said. "Otherwise you just—"

"Hey," Sandra said, "there is no point in arguing about it until we see if the guy is even interested, and I gotta get home and do my calculus homework or I'm screwed. Who needs a ride?"

Kimmy looked longingly at Sawyer.

"I'll get you a ride home," he told her in a low voice.

"I have a ride," she told Sandra happily. "I'm goin' to stay awhile and make sure Sawyer is comfortable, his arm and all," she explained.

"I'm in," Jane told Sandra. "Hey, did you get that petition together to combat those book banners?"

"I'm, like, halfway through writing it," Sandra told her. "It's got to be exactly right, you know what I mean?" She and Jane earnestly continued their conversation as they got their stuff together and walked out of the room.

"I'm outta here, too," I told Kimmy and Sawyer, getting up from the piano. I slipped the demo tape into my purse and walked over to Kimmy. "You'll see. This guy Trey is great. He's going to be a huge help to our band."

Kimmy looked at Sawyer, then back at me. "It's not *our* band, Savy. It's *your* band. You always call it *your* band."

"It's just a turn of phrase. I don't mean anything by it," I insisted.

"Oh, I wasn't criticizing you!" Kimmy cried, wide-eyed. "I would never! I just meant ... well, you still need to find my replacement."

I stared at her. "But ... if we still need to find your replacement, why did you suggest we come here to do the demo tape?"

Kimmy looked injured. "Because you're my best friend, Savy. I'd do anything for you."

"Except stay in the band," I said in a flat voice.

She didn't say a word.

"So what am I going to do?" I asked my grandmother later that night. We were sitting up together in the kitchen, drinking hot chocolate and eating her homemade oatmeal cookies. I had just explained that Kimmy was still set on quitting the band, and Jane and Sandra seemed more interested in working against the book banners than they were in Wild Hearts.

"You'll figure it out," Gramma Beth said in a distracted voice, but I didn't even notice that she wasn't her usual helpful self.

"I just don't get it," I said, pulling off a piece of a cookie and popping it into my mouth. "I would never have thought Kimmy would change her life for a guy, but she's doing it! It's like ... it's like she's become a completely different person. It's like if Sawyer says 'Jump,' she says 'How high?'"

"Um-hum," Gramma Beth said, staring into the distance.

"So, do you think I should say something to her about it?" I pressed. "Or should I wait and see what happens?"

My grandmother just stared into space.

"Gramma?"

"Huh, what?" she asked, turning to me.

"You didn't hear a word I said," I accused her.

"Oh, well, I've got some things on my mind just now," she told me. She picked up her cup and carried it to the sink, then came back and kissed me on my head. "You'll get the hang of it, Savy," she said. "You always do. Good night."

I watched her walk away and sighed. "Great, even my grandmother is blowing me off," I mumbled. There was nothing else to do but to grab a handful of cookies and head off to bed.

Once I was in my room, I put our demo tape into my Walkman and listened to it through my earphones. It was good. It was really, really good. I closed my eyes and felt the music coursing through me. I had to make something big happen for us, I just had to!

A quick look at the clock told me it was eleven, but people in the music business stayed up late, didn't they? I picked up my purse and rummaged through it until I found Trey's phone number. Then I picked up the phone and dialed.

"Trey Jackson," came his voice over the phone.

I was impressed. He sounded so professional, even at eleven o'clock at night.

"Trey? This is Savy Leeman—you heard me sing at Krissy's house?"

"Oh, sure," he said easily. "Great voice, lotsa power. So what's up?"

"I hope it's okay that I called you this late," I

said nervously, "but, well, I guess I got kind of excited. We made a demo tape."

Silence. "We?"

"Uh, remember I told you I have a band? And you said you'd listen to a demo tape?" I reminded him, feeling foolish.

"Oh, sure," he said. "Yeah, I remember. Sorry, I've got a million things on my mind right now with Jack Flash. . . . Krissy, I'm warning you, pour that crap down the sink!" he called. "Sorry, I'm in the middle of something here."

"Oh, that's okay," I assured him. "Well, the thing is, I think the tape is really good, and I was wondering if you could listen to it."

"Yeah," he said.

My heart leaped. "That would be great. When?"

"Now."

My heart did a flip-flop. "Now?"

"Yeah, well, it just occurred to me, maybe you could help me out and I could help you out. I'm having a little trouble here with Krissy. Why don't you come by, help me out with her, and I'll listen to your demo? We can kill two birds with one stone."

"What kind of trouble?" I asked him cautiously.

"You name it, she'll pop it, snort it, or drink

it." he said with disgust. "I think another girl might be able to get through to her. Right now I've just about had it, you know what I mean?"

"But Krissy is so talented!" I protested. "Maybe she just needs help!"

"No kidding," he snorted. "That's why I'm asking you to come over."

"But ... but I can't," I said. "It's a school night." I winced at my own words. A school night. How totally lame could I possibly get?

"Oh, well, yeah, I forgot, you're just a kid," Trey replied. "Never mind. So, I'll hear your tape some time or other."

I knew the big kiss-off when I heard it. I couldn't let that happen. Too much was at stake.

"Wait a minute," I said quickly. "I ... I think I can get over there. I just won't stay very long, okay?"

"Sure," Trey agreed, and briefly gave me directions to his apartment in Bellevue, which was about a fifteen-minute drive from my house.

I hung up the phone and just sat there. I would have to sneak out of the house and take the car without permission. If my parents found out, they would kill me. I would be grounded for the rest of my life. And as supportive as they were of music, they'd probably make me give up the band.

On the other hand, if I didn't do it, Trey would write me off as some stupid kid, he'd totally lose interest in Wild Hearts, and I'd probably end up losing the band anyway.

I had to go.

CHAPTER
5

$\heartsuit$

*M*y heart was pounding so loudly in my head all the way over to Trey's that I thought it could maybe burst right out of my chest. Everything looked sinister—the night, the people I passed walking their dogs, the faces in the cars next to mine. I wasn't used to doing things that my parents would kill me for doing.

It's not that I am such a super Goody Two-shoes type, not at all. The thing is, I have very nice, very cool parents. I can actually talk to them. And they actually listen—most of the time. So I really didn't need to go out and get drunk or act like a fool to prove that I was cool or grown-up or anything.

Until now.

It occurred to me that I really didn't know Trey at all. What if Krissy wasn't even at his apartment? What if he'd just told me that to lure me over there late at night? I could hear Gramma Beth calling me a sorry fool for running over to some guy's house late at night. Maybe she was right.

But no. Dustin knew Trey. And he was Jack Flash's manager! People in the music business always did things at night. Everything would be fine.

I tried very hard to talk myself into believing this.

I found Trey's apartment and walked up to the door and knocked, ready to bolt back to my car if I didn't see Krissy immediately.

The door opened, and there was Trey, holding Krissy up in his arms.

"Grab her on the other side," he instructed me.

I quickly did, looping her arm around my shoulders. She was deadweight between us. Skinny as she was, she still felt like a load.

"I came down on her hard, right after I got off the phone with you, and she got upset, went into the bathroom, and took some 'ludes," he told me, as we walked—more like dragged—Krissy around the living room.

'Ludes. I guessed he meant Quaaludes, pills that were downers, making everything slower. I had heard of them, but had never actually seen any.

"Do you think she needs to see a doctor?" I asked Trey nervously. Krissy looked terrible, white as a sheet, her sweaty hair matted to her head.

"What she needs is probably a good spanking," he snapped, adjusting Krissy's weight in his arms. "No, she's okay. I've seen her worse off than this. Besides, I know she only had about four 'ludes in her purse. I saw them."

"Huh?" Krissy mumbled, drooling out of the side of her mouth. "Wha?"

"Oh, very attractive," Trey snorted. "Let's get her into the kitchen and get some black coffee into her," he suggested. With Trey carrying most of Krissy's weight, we dragged her into the kitchen. Trey put the kettle on to boil.

"Why did she do this?" I asked, sitting at the kitchen table.

"Why does anyone do anything?" Trey asked with disgust. "I'm not a psychologist."

"I just meant . . . I mean, she's so beautiful and talented," I said softly.

"So are you," he told me, taking the kettle off the stove.

I let this compliment sink in while Trey made Krissy a cup of instant coffee. Then he sat next to her and put it to her lips. "Drink," he told her. She pulled her head away, but he forced some coffee into her mouth.

"You know, I've been through so much for this girl," Trey said softly, sounding tired. "I pay for everything for her—voice lessons, vocal coach, studio time. I even pick out her clothes and pay for them. And I don't mind, you know? At least, I didn't."

I watched the emotions playing over his handsome, troubled face as he forced more coffee into Krissy. "But I can only take so much. There's a limit."

"I can understand that," I said softly.

"That's why I had to end our personal relationship," he continued. "How many ways could I let the girl break my heart?"

I felt so bad for him, I wanted to put my arms around him. But somewhere deep inside, I was happy to hear that he and Krissy didn't have a personal relationship anymore. I had a wild urge to kiss his perfectly shaped lips, to feel his muscular arms wrapped around me. "She's throwing all her talent away," I whispered passionately.

"Yeah," Trey agreed, forcing some more coffee into Krissy. "She is. And no one can stop that but her."

"Wha?" Krissy asked, lifting her head up from her chest. Her eyes focused for a moment on Trey. "You make terrible coffee," she slurred.

He laughed a short, bitter laugh. "Too bad, because you're going to be drinking a lot of it tonight." He went to the counter and made her another cup with the still-hot water and brought it back to her.

"I can hold it," she managed to say, reaching for the coffee cup. She took a sip of the bitter coffee and looked over at me, squinting. "I know you."

"Savy," I said.

"Yeah," she agreed. "How are ya?" She drank some more of the coffee and pushed her dank hair out of her face. "I need to sleep now, Trey."

"Can you walk by yourself?" he asked her.

She got up unsteadily and walked around the small kitchen. "See?" she said, like a little girl begging for approval.

"Yeah, I see," he told her, catching her when she stumbled.

"I think I need to lie down, okay?"

"Okay," he agreed reluctantly.

She smiled at him and wove her way out of the kitchen.

"You sure she's okay?" I asked skeptically. I knew absolutely nothing about drug overdoses.

"I'm sure," Trey said, putting her coffee cup in the sink. "I've been through this with her enough times. She's taken a lot more than four 'ludes and lived to tell the tale without getting her stomach pumped. Come on, let's go into the living room. I want to hear your tape."

I handed him the tape, and he put it in an excellent sound system. He sat on the couch next to me and closed his eyes, listening intently.

I tried to listen as if I were Trey, hearing it for the first time. I felt so scared. Was it really good? Was I just dreaming? He didn't open his eyes and he didn't say one word while the tape ran through the two songs we'd demoed. Then he finally opened his eyes and looked at me.

"Huh."

I stared at him. "Is that a good 'huh' or a bad 'huh'?"

He made a little tent of his fingers and looked contemplative. "You might not want to hear what I have to say."

Oh, God, he hated us.

"No, I do," I insisted.

"You are first-rate. Your band is second-rate," he pronounced.

Well, you could have knocked me over with a feather. Wild Hearts? Second-rate?

"Are . . . are you sure?" I asked him. "I think those girls are great musicians, really."

"They're good," he allowed, "but not great. Musicians like them are a dime a dozen."

"I don't think so," I disagreed, defending my friends. "I've been playing music my whole life, and I know talent."

"Well, then, I guess you don't need me," Trey said easily, getting up and retrieving my tape. He handed it to me. "No hard feelings. Thanks for coming by. Thanks for helping with Krissy."

I held the tape in my hands, and I felt terrible. I couldn't let this happen!

"Well, maybe you could help us get better," I said.

Trey sat down and leaned toward me. "I have to work with 'great,' do you understand? There are a thousand 'goods' in this town. I don't want them. Do you get it?"

I nodded and felt tears threaten the corners of my eyes. I had been so sure that this would be our big chance. . . .

"Now, you," Trey continued earnestly, "you are great. Or at least you could be. But you'd have to leave that band."

I stood up. "Oh, no, I could never do that."

Trey stood up, too. "Why not?"

"Well, because . . . because we're a band, a team," I babbled. "We're in it together."

"Does the band mean as much to them as it

means to you?" Trey asked me in a soft, compelling voice. He took a small step toward me.

"Oh, absolutely," I lied. "The band is the most important thing for all of us."

He was standing so close to me that I could smell his cologne—some kind of musky, lemony scent—and mixed with that, something that could only be pure him. I saw that certain look in his eyes, that look I'd only ever gotten from guys I wasn't particularly interested in getting that look from. Like he liked me. Like he was interested in me. Like he wanted to kiss me.

A total "Shameless" moment, by Billy Joel. You may prefer the Garth Brooks version, but I was hearing ole Billy in my head, wailing away to beat the band.

Trey slowly reached up and smoothed some hair off my cheek. "Loyalty is a wonderful thing," he whispered. "But the music has to be the master. It has to be the only thing. Understand?"

I nodded, almost in a trance. I wanted him to kiss me and I wanted to run away, both at the same time.

"If you're interested in a real career, I can help you," Trey said. "You. Solo. No band."

"I could never do that," I said, but even to my own ears my voice sounded soft and vulnerable.

"Never say never," Trey told me, running the backs of his fingers softly down the side of my neck. "You think about it, okay?"

I wanted to just fall into his arms, but I forced myself to take a step backwards away from him. "Maybe we just need to make a better demo tape," I suggested. "Maybe if you heard us live . . ."

Trey lifted his hands, palms up, as if to say the idea was hopeless. I turned around and grabbed my purse, slinging the strap over my shoulder. I caught a glimpse of my watch. It was twelve-thirty. Nothing seemed real. Trey put his arm around me and walked me to the front door.

"Thanks for listening, anyway," I told him, stepping out the door.

He put his hand under my chin and gently kissed me. On the lips. "Hey, my pleasure," he said. "You think about what I said, okay?"

And even though I knew I would never, ever, *ever* leave Wild Hearts, I found myself nodding yes.

CHAPTER
6

I was in doo-doo so deep it's no wonder my eyes were brown.

The next day at school I was exhausted, and of course Ms. Millman called on me in American history class and I hadn't read the assigned pages. Then in the last fifteen minutes of class she pulled one of her infamous pop quizzes, which I totally flunked. I didn't have a clue.

When I handed in my quiz paper, she asked me if everything was okay, and of course I said yes. Then she said she was concerned about how much my work was slipping in her class, that if I continued on the way I was going, I was in danger of flunking. *Flunking!* My parents would kill me! I vowed to do better, and I meant it with all my heart.

At the moment.

Anyway, when I got home from school, the first thing I did was hit the history book—I was so far behind that I had to read a hundred pages to catch up. But I was so tired that I fell asleep somewhere around the Gettysburg Address, which left me eighty-three pages short on finishing my reading.

Bam-bam-bam!

I was awakened out of a deep sleep by a pounding noise, which I finally realized was someone knocking hard on my door.

"Hey, Savy, Kimmy is here!" my six-year-old brother, Timmy, called from outside the door. "Did you die in there or something?"

I padded to the door and opened it. "I just fell asleep," I told him, rubbing my tired eyes. "What time is it?"

"Six o'clock," he told me, which meant I'd been sleeping for two hours. It had seemed like two minutes.

"Kimmy's here?"

"Yeah," he replied, turning his wheelchair around with his special motorized handle. Because Timmy has juvenile rheumatoid arthritis he sometimes has to use a wheelchair, like when he's having a bad flare-up and his joints are very stiff and sore. Our house has very wide hallways and specials ramps to accommodate the chair. "Hey," he added, "when is Jane coming over?"

Timmy has had a crush on Jane from the very first day he met her.

"Soon," I said vaguely, although the truth of the matter was we didn't have a band practice scheduled.

I found Kimmy sitting in our living room, a room that is hardly ever used, because people always congregate in the family room, the kitchen, or the basement music room. She looked incongruous sitting in there, like she was waiting to be served tea or something. Gramma Beth had recently finished painting one wall peach, and various fabric swatches were pinned to that wall for consideration. The peach color clashed horribly with the yellow wall adjacent to it and with the brown sofa on which Kimmy was perched.

"Hi," I said.

She jumped up. "I know you're mad at me!" she cried, pushing her glasses up her nose. She looked like the old Kimmy I knew and loved— glasses, no makeup, baggy clothes, stringy hair. She had obviously changed after school. And even though I was the one who had instigated her makeover in the first place, I was relieved to see the old Kimmy.

"I'm not mad at you," I insisted, plopping myself down on the yellow floral love seat.

"But you hardly talked to me in school," she protested.

"That's because every time I saw you, you were with Sawyer," I pointed out.

"Well, it was his first day back at school," she replied, sitting back down on the couch. "I wanted to help him."

"Okay," I said coolly, like it was no big thing.

We just sat there, looking at each other. This wasn't like us at all. We were never at a loss for words with each other. Usually there weren't enough hours in the day for us to say everything we wanted to say.

But now it felt almost like sitting there with a stranger. Everything had changed. And I felt so sad.

"I think that demo tape we made is good," Kimmy said shyly, her cow eyes begging me to warm up to her.

"It is good," I agreed, "really good." I crossed my legs Indian-fashion. "But what difference does it make? If you leave the band, we'll have a completely different sound."

"No, you won't. You'll find someone who can play just like me."

"There isn't anyone who can play just like

you," I said bluntly. I put my legs down and leaned toward her. "I don't get it, Kimmy. I really don't. Why are you quitting?"

She looked troubled. "I ... I never wanted to be in a band," she said softly.

"Then why did you learn guitar?" I asked with exasperation, throwing my hands in the air.

"Maybe I want to play classical guitar," she said slowly.

"Kimmy, you are so full of it!" I yelled. "I'm the one who's known you forever, remember? *You're* not the one who wants to play classical guitar; it's your *parents* who want you to! You love rock and you love country, so don't give me that bull!"

"Well, maybe I don't know exactly what I want right now, okay?" she said defensively. "It's okay not to know. Right now I just want to be with Sawyer."

I jumped up from the love seat. "How can you say that? We always made fun of girls who would give up their whole life for some guy!"

Kimmy stood up, clearly distressed. "I'm not giving up my whole life! But all I know is, before Sawyer I felt like I didn't even have a life!"

Tears stung my eyes. "Well, thank you so much," I managed to say.

She reached out to touch my arm. "I didn't mean it like that. I meant ... Oh, it's so hard to explain!" She turned away from me and walked to the window, staring out at the autumn leaves slowly falling from the trees. "You of all people know how long I've been in love with Sawyer," she said, still staring outside. "I never, ever thought he'd like me back." She turned around. "And now I don't want to blow it, now that my dream has actually come true!"

I walked over to her. "But, Kimmy, if you change your life for some guy, then you're not the girl he fell for in the first place!"

She pushed her glasses up her nose. "I guess," she said. "But I can't seem to help it. All I think about is Sawyer. He's everything to me."

I knew she didn't mean it, not really. But it hurt just the same. He was everything to her. Which meant I was nothing.

"I didn't think love was supposed to make your life smaller," I said, tears threatening me. I gulped hard.

Kimmy bit her lower lip. "Don't you understand?" she said earnestly. "Sawyer could get any girl he wanted. But he wants me. Me! And I am not going to blow it!"

"Fine," I said tersely. "Don't blow it. You can

walk five paces behind him, you can do his laundry, you can ... you can breathe his air for all I care!"

"I can't stand it if you're mad at me," Kimmy said tremulously.

"Tough," I snapped. "That's just tough. I guess you know the way out."

And I turned. And then I just walked away.

Gramma Beth made her famous roast chicken for dinner, which normally I love, but I was too upset to eat. All I could think about was Kimmy. We'd had our first real fight. I was losing my best friend. And I just didn't know what to do about it.

Neither of my older brothers were home for dinner, but everyone else was there, talking and laughing and carrying on, per usual. Timmy told a funny story about his teacher, and my little sister, Shelly, went on and on about the finals for her school spelling bee.

"And how about you, Savy?" my mother asked, as she helped Magenta Sue, our housekeeper—whose real ambition is to be the next Pam Tillis—clear the table.

"What?" I asked. I had been lost in thought, trying to figure out what to do about Kimmy. I felt terrible about walking out on her that way.

"How's school? How's the band?" my mom asked.

"Everything is okay," I answered noncommittally. I really didn't want to get into it at the dinner table. I snuck a look over at Gramma Beth, who is very blunt and would have been the first one to call me on this lie. But Gramma Beth looked as lost in thought as I had just been, and she didn't say a word.

"You haven't had a band practice for a few days," my dad noted. "Y'all still planning to enter that Battle of the Bands at Vanderbilt?"

"Maybe," I replied.

His eyebrows shot up.

"It's kind of complicated," I mumbled.

"Why don't you ask the girls to come on over on Sunday and play some music with us?" my mother suggested. Sunday afternoon is usually family music time at our house, where we all get together and jam in the basement. Sometimes various friends sit in and play with us. It's actually really, really fun. Usually.

"They're busy," I said.

My parents exchanged a look. I knew what they were thinking: Where is our daughter, Miss Enthusiasm? But I didn't feel like faking it, and I was too bummed out to care.

"Can I be excused?" I asked, just as Magenta Sue was bringing the strawberry shortcake to the table.

"All right," my mother said. I got up, and she caught my hand as I went by her chair. "Are you sure you're okay, baby?" she asked me.

"Sure," I told her. "I'm fine."

But I wasn't fine. I felt awful. I had to call Kimmy and make things right. I went to my room and quickly dialed her private number.

"Hi, this is Kimmy," her taped voice said in her soft drawl. "I'm not at home right now. Please leave a message."

I couldn't leave a message. What could I say?

Maybe she was home, but she just wasn't in her room so she couldn't hear the phone. I dialed her mother's number.

"Carrier residence," came the voice of Mrs. Gruller, Kimmy's mother's assistant.

"Hey, Mrs. Gruller, it's Savy," I said. "Is Kimmy there?"

"No, honey, she isn't," Mrs. Gruller said. "Mr. Gruller just drove her over to Sawyer's house."

That figured.

"Did you want to leave a message for her?" Mrs. Gruller continued. "You can call on her phone and leave it, or I can take it for you."

"No, that's okay," I said. "Thanks, anyway," and I hung up and threw myself down on my bed. I just felt so tired.

The phone rang.

"Hello?"

"Hi, it's Trey." His voice sounded so low and sexy over the phone.

"Hi," I said, sitting up on my bed.

"Listen, I know this is last minute, but Jack Flash is in the studio tonight. We're doing a demo at Aces. I thought you might like to come sit in."

Aces recording studio! It was a famous recording studio on Music Row—state-of-the-art—where people like Garth Brooks and Travis Tritt and Pam Tillis recorded their albums. I had only been inside it once, on a class trip with all the kids in All-State choir the year before. But to sit in on an actual recording session, with Trey.

Woah, baby!

"I'd love to!" I exclaimed, not bothering to try to mute my excitement. Suddenly I didn't feel tired at all. "When should I come?"

"About ten," he told me. "That good for you?"

"Absolutely," I assured him. "I'll be there. Thanks for the invite!"

"No problem," he said easily. "I'll see you there."

I hung up the phone, filled with anticipation. Maybe Trey was reconsidering about Wild Hearts! Or maybe ... maybe he liked me. Really liked me. Liked me maybe as a Girlfriend with a capital *G*.

Naaaaaah.

But ... maybe. I closed my eyes and remembered the way he had looked at me the night before. I got a little shiver, thinking about how his fingers had felt on my neck.

A college guy. A really, really cute, cool, smart college guy.

Take that, Kimmy.

I had to get the car. I just had to. And I wasn't about to risk sneaking out again. No way could I get away with it two nights in a row. I went to find my parents, who were in the family room staining some furniture.

"Can I take one of the cars?" I asked them.

My father looked at his watch. "Where did you want to go?"

"I've been invited to a professional recording session at Aces studio!" I explained with excitement.

"Well, that is exciting," my mom said, a grin on her face. "Who invited you?"

"Trey Jackson," I replied. "He's a friend of Dustin's, and he manages this rock group called Jack Flash. I've never been to a professional recording session."

"Well, at the risk of stating the obvious, I have to remind you that you've got homework to finish," my mother said, dipping her brush back into the can of stain.

"I know, but this is such an opportunity," I gushed. "Please say I can go, please!"

They exchanged another one of their patented parent looks. I swear, my parents can communicate by telepathy.

"If you finish all your homework, you can go for one hour," my father finally said. "Deal?"

"Deal!" I cried, giving him a hard hug.

This is what I mean about my parents being cool. Someone else's parents would have just insisted that because it would be too late, the kid couldn't go. But my parents knew how important this would be to me, and so they said yes.

I ran over to hug my mother. "Thanks! I love you!"

My mother laughed. "Well, we're happy to see the old Savy back. Who was that long-faced stranger at the dinner table?"

81

"My seriously depressed evil twin!" I said, laughter spilling over. I ran for my room to figure out what to wear.

I was so psyched! And I had so much to do to get ready!

That part about finishing all my homework before I left somehow completely fled from my mind.

CHAPTER
7

CHAPTER 7

walked into Aces recording studio, and it was like walking into my dreams.

The lobby had forest green carpeting and cherry-wood furniture. Hanging plants competed for wall space with blowups of CD covers from artists who had recorded there. Through the glass I could see into the soundproof recording room, where Jack Flash was in the middle of a number. The sound system was on, and their music was carried throughout the studio. Trey was standing in the engineer's booth with the sound engineer, intently listening to the mix. The engineer would move this lever or that on his mixing board, adjusting the sound.

I figured I should wait until the song finished to get Trey's attention, so I just stood there, watching Krissy and the band do their song. Krissy did a long, gospel-tainted riff that was incredible, but then she stumbled backwards and practically fell into Ryan, who had danced over behind her during the bridge of the song.

"Cut, cut, cut!" Trey called into the mike that fed into the studio room. "What was that?"

The band stopped playing and just stood there, mostly looking ticked off. Trey stormed into the studio, so I couldn't hear him anymore. But I could see him. He was yelling at Krissy, gesticulating wildly, pointing a finger in her face. She put her hands on her hips defensively and shook her head no. Then Trey reached down to the floor and picked up the glass of brownish liquid she'd been drinking, which looked to be Coke. Trey tasted it, and then he went nuts again. He took the drink with him and marched back into the sound booth, where he set the drink down hard, some of it sloshing over onto the floor. Krissy looked at him defiantly through the glass and said something nasty under her breath.

"Take ten," he called through the mike. Then he ran his hand through his hair and came out into the lobby. That's when he saw me.

"Hi," I said, feeling awkward, like maybe I shouldn't be there.

"Hi," he said, giving me a meltingly cute smile. "I'm glad to see a friendly face." He came over to me and gave me a little kiss on the cheek. "It's not usually like this. . . . Well, then again, lately maybe it is." He sighed and ran his hand through his hair again. "This studio time costs a mint, and Krissy's been messing up. I asked her not to drink, but it seems she's been sneaking rum into her Coke for the past two hours." He paced the room, as if he couldn't bear to be still; then he came back over to me and looked me over appraisingly. "Anyway, you look cute. And healthy, I might add."

I was glad I'd taken so much time to get ready. I had on a black and white checked full skirt that came about an inch above my knees, with black cowboy boots. On top I wore a sleeveless white T-shirt with a black suede vest and a black jean jacket.

"What are you doing here?" Krissy asked, marching over to us.

I was taken aback at the anger in her voice. "Trey invited me."

"Well, isn't that ducky," she seethed. I could tell she was kind of drunk by the way she was slurring her words.

Trey turned to her. "Did you just go have a drink in the john?" he asked her.

"What if I did?" She put her hands on her hips belligerently, but then she saw the look on his face, like he was ready to kill her, and she backed down. "Look, I sing better when I've been drinking. I can control it, you know. You don't have to baby-sit me."

"That's exactly what I have to do," Trey seethed. "Someone has to."

"I only drink because of those pills," Krissy whined. "They make me so nervous—"

Trey grabbed Krissy's arm and pulled her away from me. "I told you not to take those anymore."

"But I have to," she said, tears pooling in her eyes. "I'll get fat otherwise!"

Trey dropped her arm and looked defeated. "I'll go get you some coffee." He walked down the hall to a vending machine.

Krissy looked at me. "You're after my boyfriend, aren't you?" she said bluntly.

"N-no," I stammered. "I—"

"I'd watch it, if I were you," she said darkly. Then she turned and stumbled away.

Wow. She was one messed-up girl.

Was I after her boyfriend?

But no, Trey wasn't her boyfriend anymore. He'd told me that himself.

"Hi. You're Savy, right?"

It was Ryan, the bass player. He walked up to

me sipping on a soda and munching from a small bag of chips, which he held out to me.

"No, thanks," I said.

"Trey invite you here?" he asked me.

"Yeah." I looked at my watch. Almost a half hour had already passed. At the rate they were going, I'd have to leave before I even got to see how the studio really worked.

"I'd watch out for him," Ryan said conversationally.

"What is that supposed to mean?" I replied irritably.

Ryan shrugged. "It's just ... well, you seem like a really nice girl. Normal."

"And?"

"And Trey can be ... difficult," Ryan said, finishing the bag of chips.

"Look, I don't know what you're talking about," I told him. "And I don't want to get in the middle of the stuff going on with your band, okay?"

"No one's asking you to," Ryan said. "I was trying to tell you something as a friend. A potential friend."

Trey came running over to us. "Damn, we're gonna have to cancel the rest of the session. Krissy's in the bathroom, and she's out cold."

"Should I go see if she's okay?" I asked.

"No, I already went in there," Trey said. "I've gotta talk to the engineer and see if I can get out of paying for the next two hours—which is probably hopeless." He looked at me. "Will you wait for me?"

"Sure," I said. Trey ran off.

Ryan shook his head. "Man, this is messed up. Really, really messed up."

"How can Krissy keep throwing her chances away like this?" I wondered.

Ryan gave me a hard look. "Savy, no offense, but you don't know anything about it."

"I know self-destructiveness when I see it," I said. "I'm going to check on Krissy."

I went into the ladies' room and found Krissy nodding out on a little couch. I got some of the icky brown paper towels from the machine, wet them, and held them against her forehead.

"I'm really sorry, Trey," she mumbled when I held the cold compress on her. "I know you hate me now."

"It isn't Trey," I whispered.

But she didn't hear me. She just passed out again.

Trey came and found us, and together we hauled Krissy out of the studio and into his car.

"Come with me?" he pleaded.

"I have to get home—"

"Please?" he asked. "The whole band just ran out. They're sick of dealing with her. I just . . . It would really mean a lot to me if you'd come."

What could I do?

We drove Krissy home, not speaking; then he lifted her up and carried her into her house while I waited in the car. When he came back, he got in and put his head down on the steering wheel.

I touched the back of his head, and he grabbed my hand and held it fast.

"I can't do this anymore," he whispered. He lifted his head, and his eyes looked red and sad. "I can't save her."

"She has to save herself, I guess," I said.

"I had such big dreams for her. . . ."

"Maybe you could help her get into a rehab program or something."

He laughed bitterly. "Yeah, like I haven't tried. She's just bent on self-destruction."

He was still holding my hand. Slowly he brought it up to his lips, turned it over, and kissed my palm. "Thanks for being there, Savy."

"You're welcome."

"God, you're like a breath of fresh air," he mused. "So . . . so normal! And you're so talented." He put his arm across the back of the seat, leaning close to me. "I could do wonderful things for you. I really believe that."

"For my band?" I asked him, not willing to relinquish hope.

"For you," he insisted. "I'm killing myself with Krissy, and she doesn't even appreciate what I've done for her. She's addicted to pills and booze—she's a mess. Let me manage you."

"But my band—" I protested.

"So stay with your band," he interrupted. "You can do both! Just because we're working on your solo career doesn't mean you can't be in your band, does it?"

"I guess not," I agreed. I had never thought of that before. "But what about Jack Flash? You can't just give up on Krissy."

"I tell you what," Trey said, excitement edging into his voice. "I won't give up on Krissy, and you won't quit your band, but you and I can start working together. Then everyone gets everything, and no one suffers. What do you think?"

"I think . . . I think I have to think about it," I replied.

Trey moved closer to me. I could feel his hand on the back of my neck, rubbing the tension away. "I really want to do this," he said softly. "And I think it's what you really want, too."

I thought about Jane and Sandra, who were both so busy that the band seemed to be second or third on their list of priorities. And I thought about Kimmy, who didn't have any loyalty to the band at all.

So what was stopping me? How could I let a chance like this pass me by? But still, something about it made me feel funny. I had to talk to someone, get another opinion, before I agreed. Which was just what I told Trey.

"I understand," he said, moving away from me. "But don't take too long. Sometimes if you don't jump onto a fast-moving train, it moves on to the next stop without you."

The next stop. Some other girl's career.

I knew I had to make a decision fast, or it would be too late.

Gramma Beth was up, sitting at the kitchen table drinking tea when I tiptoed into the house. It was twelve-thirty.

"Am I dead meat?" I asked her.

She stirred her tea. "Well, since I told your parents I'd be up and they could go to sleep, I guess they don't know just what time you up and decided to mosey in."

"There were extenuating circumstances," I said, sitting down next to her.

She sipped her hot tea. "I'm listening."

So I told her all about Krissy and how she passed out from drugs and liquor and how I helped Trey get her home and how he wanted to manage my career.

"How do you feel about it?" she asked me.

"Confused," I admitted. "Like I really, really want to, but then something kind of stops me."

"What's the part that's stopping you?" she asked.

I ran my finger over the grain of the table as I tried to figure it out. "I guess it makes me feel . . . disloyal. To my band."

"Doesn't have to be that way," Gramma Beth said.

"You think?"

"It's not what I think that matters; it's what you think," she replied. "But maybe what you need to do is to talk it over with Kimmy and Jane and Sandra. It's only gonna be a poison if you do something behind their backs."

"Yeah, I guess that's right," I agreed. "Maybe they'll even encourage this, huh?"

"Kimmy called you right after you left," Gramma Beth said. "She said you should call her, no matter what time you got home. She said it was very important, and you shouldn't forget, no matter what."

I got up. "Thanks, Gramma," I said, kissing her cheek. "I'm sorry I was late. You won't tell?"

"Not as long as you don't start making a habit

of it," she replied. "I'll say something nice and vague without actually lying."

I walked to the doorway and turned back to her. "You're the best. I don't know what I'd do without you."

To my surprise tears came to my grandmother's eyes. Now, trust me when I tell you my grandmother is not a crier. She can be a yeller. She's a laugher, big-time. And she's definitely a doer. But she is not a crier.

"You're a strong girl, Savy," she said. "I don't worry about you."

"Are you okay?" I asked her.

"Sometimes I worry about Dustin," she said, as if she hadn't heard me. "He's a dreamer, you know."

"Gramma?"

"He's such a tender soul, he could get hurt," she continued, staring off into space. "Timmy will be fine, and Shelly—she's got steel under all that sweetness, you mark my words. Dylan will be okay. But Dustin—"

"Gramma, what are you talking about?" I asked her in a loud voice, fear crawling up my arms.

She finally focused on me. "Oh, nothing, sweet pea. I'm just a-rambling. Don't pay me no never mind. Go on to bed. And call Kimmy."

Weird. Very weird.

I tiptoed down the hall to my room and quickly dialed Kimmy's number, hoping she wasn't already asleep.

"Savy?" she said when she snatched up the phone after the first ring.

"I guess no one else would be calling you this late, huh?"

"I'm so glad you called," she said. "I tried to call you as soon as I got home from Sawyer's house, and I've just been sitting here hoping you'd call me back."

"Are you okay?"

"No," she said. "Because I can't stand that we had a fight! We never fight!"

"I know," I said, sitting heavily on my bed. "I hated it too."

"Let's make up right now, okay?" she asked me anxiously. "Because I can't even sleep or anything until I know we're not fighting."

"I notice you were able to make it over to Sawyer's house," I pointed out, "so you couldn't have been too distraught."

"But I was," she insisted. "I told him all about it. He's so great. He said I should call you right away."

"That's why you called me?" I asked her. "Because your boyfriend told you to?"

"Well, no," she said defensively. "I already wanted to. It's just that I realized how right he was. Aren't you glad I called?"

"Yeah, I am," I admitted. I wrapped the phone cord around my finger. "Listen, what would you think if someone—someone professional— wanted to manage my singing career?"

"Well, I think that would be good," Kimmy said slowly. "I know how important music is to you."

"It used to be that important to you, too," I reminded her sadly.

Silence.

"Savy, when you're in love, you'll understand," she finally said softly. "Everything changes."

We said good night and I hung up the phone. I should have felt happy that Kimmy was encouraging me to work with Trey, but instead, for some reason, I just felt like crying.

And as clear as the stars in the night sky I could hear this sad old Stevie Wonder song, "Everything Must Change," as it wrapped around me and finally lulled me off to sleep.

CHAPTER
8

What is all this?" I asked Trey, scanning the list he had just handed me. It was Monday evening. I spent the weekend trying to figure out what I wanted to do. Then at lunch that day I'd called Trey from school and told him I wanted him to manage my singing career. We'd agreed to meet at Musical Burgers at six o'clock, in the back booth under the neon dancing-burger clock.

I had spent two hours after school studying. Ms. Millman had told me that if I didn't do better on my next history test, she was going to ask my parents to come in to speak with her—that's how concerned she was about me. Well, I couldn't let that happen, so I swore up and down to her that

I'd start studying and bring up my grade. But you can only get so much done in two hours. I had to write a short paper for English, for example, and that took one hour all by itself. I did manage to read about half of what I needed to read to catch up in history. At least it was a start.

Anyway, school was the last thing on my mind as I sat there with Trey, staring at the list he had just handed me.

"It's your schedule," he explained, moving the menu out of the way so he could reach for it. "Mondays from five to six you have vocal coaching with Peter Jergenson, Wednesdays from four to five you have a voice lesson with Sarah Carlton—"

"She's the one who works with Krissy, isn't she?" I interrupted.

"Because she's the best," Trey said. "I only want the very best for you."

"How did you arrange this so fast?" I wondered.

Trey grinned. "It's my job."

"But ... but I can't afford this," I explained hesitantly.

"You don't have to 'afford' anything," Trey said. "I pay for it and charge it against your future earnings."

I pushed some hair behind my ear. "What earnings?"

"Okay, here's how it works," Trey said. "You get a deal with, say, Warner Brothers. You start making money. We keep track of everything I spend to get you to that point, and then you pay me back out of your earnings."

"I guess that makes sense," I agreed. "And you take a percentage of what I make?"

"Twenty percent," Trey said firmly.

My eyebrows shot up. "I had always heard it was ten or fifteen percent," I said.

"Yeah," Trey agreed, "but no other manager would put money out for you now, or take you on when your career is nowhere, right?"

"I guess," I said. I looked back down at the list. "What's six o'clock to seven o'clock every day?" I asked him. "It's marked W.O."

"Work out," Trey translated. "There's an early bird advanced aerobics class at the Sweat Shoppe on Hillsboro Road. You can make it and still get to school on time."

I stared at him in horror. "I'm supposed to get up at five o'clock in the morning every day and go work out before school?"

Trey nodded calmly.

"But I'm not a morning person!" I exclaimed. "I wouldn't even know my name that early in the morning!"

Trey's face hardened. "You want to take this seriously or not?"

"I do, but—"

"Because if you don't, I can move right on to some other girl who would appreciate this—"

"No, no," I assured him. "I can do it."

Trey smiled and took my hand across the table. "I'm doing this for you. Your look is just as important as your sound. And you know I think you're great-looking, but ..." Trey hesitated.

"What?" I asked him.

"Well, don't take this the wrong way, but you need to take off ten pounds.... No, more like twenty."

I pulled my hand back. "But I'm not that fat!"

"No," Trey agreed, "but you're ... round. Your face still has that baby-fat look. Girls with baby fat don't become stars, do they?"

"I guess not," I agreed reluctantly.

"Ya'll ready to order?" the waitress asked, coming over to our booth.

I recognized her from last Saturday. It was Bettina, the wanna-be singer. Her face lit up when she recognized me.

"Hey, you're in that band, Wild Girls, aren't you?" she asked me.

"Wild Hearts," I corrected her.

"So did ya'll have time to listen to my tape?" she asked me hopefully.

"Gee, sorry," I said kindly. "We didn't." I

turned to Trey. "Bettina is a singer. This is Trey Jackson, my manager," I added proudly.

"You're a manager?" she asked.

Trey nodded.

Bettina reached into the pocket of her apron and pulled out one of her demo tapes. "Well, if you ever have time to give this a listen, it would mean the world to me. I'm really good."

She gave Trey a flirtatious smile, and it seemed to me he was looking her over contemplatively.

"Thanks," he said, slipping the tape into his pocket. "I'll listen to it."

"Thanks!" Bettina said, her face alive with hope and happiness. "My phone number is right on there, so you can call me. Anytime," she added.

Jeez, she was shameless.

"So, are you two ready to order?" she asked us, pencil poised.

"I'll have a cheeseburger and fries and a diet Coke," I told her.

Trey gave me a dark look and mouthed the words "baby fat" at me.

"On second thought," I said slowly, "I'll have a small salad—"

"No dressing," Trey put in.

"No dressing," I repeated, "and the diet Coke."

Trey beamed his approval and ordered a grilled cheese and tomato sandwich and black coffee.

"This is supposed to be dinner," I said after Bettina left the table. I figured Trey thought I was ordering that cheeseburger as a snack, and that was why he'd stopped me. "I mean, I told my family I wouldn't be home to eat because you said we'd have this meeting over dinner."

"You just ordered dinner, didn't you?" Trey asked easily.

"A small salad, no dressing? My little brother Timmy's pet gerbil eats more than that."

"Your little brother Timmy's pet gerbil doesn't want to be a star," Trey pointed out. He took Bettina's tape out of his pocket and turned it over in his hands, then put it away again.

I got the message. It didn't have to be me he was helping—that was what he seemed to be saying. It could be Bettina. I caught a glimpse of her across the restaurant. Under that disheveled appearance she was thin and blond and had great cheekbones.

A fast-moving train. Some other girl's career. These were the thoughts that ran through my mind.

Okay, probably I would look better if I were thinner. And working out would be good for me.

I didn't see how I could possibly have time for Wild Hearts or my homework or my friends or my family. But somehow I would have to work it out.

"Hi, Savy, it's Jane," came her voice through the phone.

It was a week later, after school, and I'd been trying to study but had fallen asleep. Getting up so early to go to that aerobics class was killing me. Also, I was living on next to no food. I thought about sneaking food when I wasn't with Trey, but he started weighing me in every night. Whenever I was home for dinner, I pushed the food around on my plate so it would look as if I'd eaten something. Fortunately I had only been home for three dinners, and my parents were at a meeting for one of those. I mean, they aren't stupid. Eventually they were going to catch on. But I couldn't think about that. I was starving and irritable, but I had lost three pounds. Every time I fell asleep, though, I dreamed about Gramma Beth's cooking.

"Oh, hi," I said sleepily, trying to wake up. "What's up?"

"You sound like you're in zombie land," Jane said. "You okay?"

"I fell asleep," I told her, trying to clear my head.

"You sick or something?" Jane asked me.

"No, just a headache," I lied. I didn't have a headache. I had an everywhere-ache. Every part of my body hurt from that stupid exercise class. The women in it were like something out of a science-fiction TV show—superwomen with muscles on their muscles.

I hadn't told anyone that I was getting up at five o'clock in the morning to go to an aerobics class. Actually, I hadn't said anything at all about my arrangement with Trey. All I'd ever done was pose that question to Kimmy in theory.

Sue me, I was a wuss. I was afraid they would hate me.

"Listen," Jane said, "I got my schedule at Uncle Zap's for next week. I practically had to give birth at a stupid staff meeting to get some free nights, but I got them. So you want to plan band practice?"

Free nights. I didn't have any free nights. I was supposed to meet with Trey every night to pick out material and work on it.

"Uh, maybe we should check with Sandra," I said evasively.

"I just called her," Jane reported. "She told her tennis coach she needed time for her band. The only thing we've got is a meeting next Wednesday at four about how to deal with those idiots who want to burn books. You should come."

Wednesday at four. I had a voice lesson with Ms. Carlton.

"Maybe," I said noncommittally.

"You sound major weird, girlfriend, I gotta tell you," Jane stated. "Are you sure you're not sick?"

"Maybe," I said grasping at an excuse. "Maybe I'm getting the flu."

"Well, ask Gramma Beth to make you some chicken soup," Jane suggested. "My best friend from New York, Anita Lebowitz, swears it can cure anything."

Chicken soup. Oh, God. Fragrant chicken soup with my grandmother's homemade matzo balls, carrots and celery swimming in the golden broth and—

"Yo, Savy, you there?" Jane called.

"Yeah."

"So, you want to call Kimmy, or should I?"

"You can," I said listlessly. I had barely talked to Kimmy for the past week.

"Well, okay," Jane agreed, sounding doubtful. "Listen, get some rest. You sound like you're on some bizarro drugs or something. You're not, are you?"

"Of course not," I said. "I'm okay."

"If you say so," Jane said. "Later." She hung up.

I turned over on my bed and stared at the ceiling. I was so tired and so hungry, and I'd only been on this stupid regimen for a week. But I honestly didn't know if I could take it.

"Savy! Dinner!" Shelly called.

Dinner. Another meal where I'd have to fool my family into thinking I was eating.

"Pot roast, your favorite," Magenta Sue said happily as she carried some serving plates to the table. I got the salad from the sideboard and put it on the table. It was all I was actually going to eat anyway. Joy.

My older brothers, Dustin and Dylan, were actually home for dinner for a change. Everyone passed the food around and began to eat hungrily. I nibbled the tiniest edge of a golden brown potato and mushed the rest of it into the meat.

"Hey, I saw Trey at school today. He told me he's working with you," Dustin said as he helped himself to extra potatoes.

My family looked at me with interest. I hadn't exactly filled them in on my relationship with Trey. I'd just said a friend was helping me with my career. The only one who knew was Gramma Beth, and she'd keep a secret to her grave.

"Sort of," I said, stabbing a lettuce leaf with my fork.

"He's the friend you told us about?" Dad asked.

I nodded and drank some water. "It's an informal thing, you know?"

"He's a pretty intense guy," Dustin warned. "I want you to be careful."

"You're not my father," I snapped. Everyone looked at me as if I'd lost my mind. "I mean," I said, forcing myself to relax, "it's no big thing."

"I don't know," Dustin said. "I heard that Trey was a really bad influence on Krissy—you know, the singer from Jack Flash."

"Well, I am not Krissy," I replied. "I don't do drugs and I don't drink. Krissy is Krissy's problem, that's what I think."

"I've heard bad stuff about him, too," Dylan put in.

Great. My big brothers were ganging up on me.

"Such as?" my mother asked.

"Such as that he was the one who—" Dylan began. Then he caught my eye, and he stopped. "It was probably nothing," he finished.

"He was the one who what, son?" my father asked.

"It was just a rumor," Dylan mumbled. "Is there any more pot roast?"

Just then Timmy spilled his milk, the phone rang, and Shelly started telling a story about her basketball team, so we dropped the subject of Trey. One of the good things about having a really big family is that your personal life can get lost in the shuffle when you really want it to.

The funny thing was, nothing, but nothing, got by my grandmother. And though it didn't even occur to me at the time, she just sat there, and she never said a word.

CHAPTER 9

*I*t was the next day, after school, and this is what I was thinking: if my life is going so great, why do I feel so awful?

Well, let's see, for a lot of reasons. First of all, Ms. Millman was now insisting that one or both of my parents come to school to see her. I was basically flunking history. I had tried desperately to talk her out of this drastic stance, but she would not be swayed. So I promised I'd tell my parents. But I hadn't said a word. I knew we were having another quiz the next day. My plan was to study so hard that I would ace it, and then Ms. Millman would forget all about how she'd wanted to meet with my parents.

My grade in basic chemistry wasn't much better than my history grade. I figured it was only a matter of time until Mr. Mooring—whom we all called Mr. Boring, for obvious reasons—wanted my parents to come in and see him, too. I was doing okay in the rest of my classes, but that's because I'm smart and they came easily to me. I just didn't have time to do homework.

Second of all, Wild Hearts was practically at a total standstill. And it wasn't the other girls' fault; it was mine. There just weren't enough hours in the day to do everything I had to do. We had only had one band practice, and it had been a halfhearted session where we didn't accomplish much. I pleaded the flu, but I was a stone-cold liar.

Lying to my family and to my best friends is not the greatest feeling in the world, let me tell you.

Of course, there was a major upside. I had lost four pounds; I was beginning to see actual cheekbones in my face. My singing was better than ever. And the songs Trey was finding for me were just incredible. He kept telling me I could really, truly be a star, and I was really, truly beginning to believe it.

Anyway, I was lying on my bed, my history book open in front of me, trying to stay awake long enough to read chapters ten through twelve, when the phone rang.

"Savy, it's for you!" Shelly yelled down the hall.

I picked up the phone. "Hello?"

"Hi, it's me," Trey said. "I need a huge favor."

I sat up. "What?"

"I'm over at the Big Bamboo with Jack Flash. We're supposed to be doing a sound check for our gig tonight, and Krissy is already completely out of it."

"You can sober her up," I said. I looked at my watch. "It's only five o'clock."

"No, you don't understand," Trey explained, an edge to his voice. "I mean really out of it. Like nuts. She showed up an hour late, drunk and stoned on who knows what, and then when I called her on it she had a fit and went storming out of here. I don't even know where she is."

"She wasn't driving, was she?" I asked, immediately concerned that she could kill herself or someone else.

"No. Ryan said some guy was waiting for her out in front in a red Miata convertible," Trey said. "Look, Savy, you gotta help me out here."

"What can I do?"

"You gotta sing with Jack Flash tonight," Trey said.

"I *what*?"

"You heard me," Trey said. "You have to do it."

"But ... but I can't!" I cried. "If I don't study history tonight, I'm gonna flunk! And anyway, I don't know their stuff! It's not my band! I don't sound anything like Krissy! I—"

"Hey, hey, take a deep breath," Trey interrupted. "One obstacle at a time. First of all, you need to know how important this is. Jack Flash is opening for Prairie Fire tonight. Prairie Fire just got signed to RCA, so all the biggies in town are gonna be here tonight to check them out."

"But, Trey, I—"

"Second of all," Trey continued, "if you get over here now, you can go over Jack Flash's charts. You're a great sight reader, and about half of the tunes they do are cover tunes you know, anyway. Third of all, it doesn't matter if you don't sound like Krissy. You sound like you, which is dynamite."

I sighed heavily into the phone. "How can I sing with another band?" I finally said. "I mean, I have a band—"

"I'm not asking you to join their band, dammit!" Trey exploded. "I'm asking you for a favor. I think I do enough for you to ask for a favor! If I don't have a singer tonight, the band is gonna have to cancel. Do you want that on your head?"

"No," I said meekly.

"I knew you wouldn't," Trey said. "So what time can you get here?"

"In an hour, I guess," I said, half in a daze. "But ... isn't there someone else? If I don't stay home and study, I—"

"Savy, if I knew another singer as good as you, I would be managing her instead of you," Trey said in a hard voice. "Now, are you gonna get serious about this, or do I find another singer?"

"No, I'm serious," I assured him.

"Good," Trey said. "Be here in thirty minutes. I knew I could count on you."

He hung up before I could ask him what I should wear and what if I couldn't get the car and a million other questions that were flying through my brain.

Okay. I had to make a plan. First I had to get a car. And I would take my history book with me and study whenever I had time, like after the sound check and between sets. I would just have to make it work.

I found my brother Dustin watching CNN in the family room.

"I need a huge favor," I said, sitting on the cushioned arm of his chair.

"What?"

"Are you staying home tonight?" I asked him.

"Yeah, I've got to write a paper for my music comp class, why?"

I took a deep breath. "I need to borrow your car."

"What for?" Dustin asked, muting the sound on the TV with the remote control.

"Just . . . something I need to do," I said, feeling irritated. Before he had his own car he didn't want to have to answer to Mom and Dad about where he was going all the time. And I sure didn't want to have to answer to my brother!

"Use Mom's car," he said.

"No, she's at the women's shelter doing volunteer work tonight," I reminded him. "And Dad is going to The Box Seat to watch a hockey game."

"Ask Gramma Beth," he said.

"I don't want to ask Gramma Beth!" I cried.

"How come?"

He was really starting to pain me. "Because Gramma Beth would worm the truth out of the devil and I don't want to tell her where I'm going, okay?" I yelled.

"You don't tell me, you don't get my car," Dustin said implacably, and he clinked the sound back on the TV.

Oh, just great. If I told Dustin, he'd give me another lecture about Trey, which I could gladly do without. And then after he gave me the lec-

ture, he'd say I couldn't use his car anyway.
Dylan had a car too, but he wasn't home.

I ran to my room to check my cash situation.
I had three dollars in my purse and about five
more dollars in quarters in a dish on my dresser.

Well, there was only one solution. I would have
to take a taxi, and Trey would have to pay for it
when I got there.

I jumped into the shower and quickly dressed
in a long flowered dress that buttoned down the
front. I put on some makeup, slipped into my
clogs, and called a taxi, my heart pounding in
my chest.

I was breaking so many parental rules that it
made me dizzy. Like I couldn't go out on school
nights. Like I had to tell my parents where I was
going. Like I wasn't allowed in the Big Bamboo
because I was underage. On and on and on.

I told the taxi driver to pick me up on the
corner in fifteen minutes. Then I quickly dialed
Kimmy's number.

Please be home, I prayed to myself. Please
don't be at Sawyer's.

I lucked out. Kimmy answered the phone.

"I need your help," I blurted out.

"Anything!" she said earnestly. "What?"

But I couldn't tell her that I was singing with
Jack Flash. I just couldn't. "I have a date with

Trey Jackson, that college guy I told you about,"
I invented. I had made up a story that I was
dating this college guy, which was why I was so
busy and so tired. I knew it was stupid to lie, but
I did it anyway. "I need to sneak out of the
house. But I need a cover story. So can I say I'm
at your house?"

"Sure," Kimmy said. "But won't they see
Trey's car when he picks you up?"

"I told him to meet me at the corner," I fibbed,
hating every lying word that was coming out of
my mouth. "So will you cover for me?"

"Of course," Kimmy promised. "Just call me
when you get back home from your date so I
know, okay?"

"Okay," I agreed, feeling relieved. "Thanks."

I pulled a piece of stationery out of my drawer,
and quickly scribbled a note, saying I was at Kimmy's. Then I stuck the note on my door with a
thumbtack. I picked up my purse and my history
book, and like a low-down lying thief, I snuck
out the back door.

Desperado. The Eagles. Seriously.

"Just remember, you're twenty-two," Trey
kept telling me backstage at the Big Bamboo.

I nodded and paced, sweat making rivers down
my spine and under my arms, cementing my flo-

ral-print dress to my body. I had never been so nervous in my life. Lying about my age so I wouldn't get busted was just one of my many concerns. Fortunately, the club manager hadn't auditioned the band, so he didn't know I wasn't the regular lead singer for Jack Flash. Trey told me he'd been out when Krissy showed up earlier. And it just never occurred to him that a hot rock band that played clubs around Nashville would have an underage lead singer.

The guys in Jack Flash were really nice and supportive, going over all their tunes with me. Ryan was especially kind, always encouraging me and trying to build up my confidence. In some dim part of my mind I thought what a nice guy he was and how he seemed to like me. But I was too busy freaking out over everything else in my life to give him too much thought.

I was able to learn six of their original tunes, which I would do with the lead sheets (they have the melody, lyrics, and guitar chords on them), open in front of me on a music stand. Other than that, we were going to do all cover tunes that I already knew. Well, supposedly. I was so nervous I didn't know what I knew anymore.

And forget about opening my history book. I tried once, but it was just words swimming around on a piece of paper.

We were set to go on in ten minutes. At that moment I couldn't remember the words to one song. Not one. Ryan came up to me and handed me a paper cup of water.

"Thanks," I said, and took a sip. I stared at him bleakly. "I do not remember anything," I said.

He put his arm around me and gave me a hug. "You will," he assured me. "You'll be great."

"I will?" I was desperate for reassurance.

"Absolutely," he said.

Trey came bursting into the dressing room. He looked me over. "Aren't you changing?"

I looked down at myself. "Into what?"

"Into Krissy," Ryan said under his breath.

Trey turned to him. "I don't need to take any crap from you tonight, got it?"

"Yeah, I guess the truth hurts, huh?" Ryan said angrily.

"You don't know what you're talking about," Trey snapped.

Ryan just shook his head sadly and walked away. Trey turned back to me.

"You ... you didn't tell me what to wear," I faltered.

"Something sexy would have been a good idea," Trey said in a scathing voice. "You look like a chubby flower child in that thing."

"Well, sorry," I said, feeling defensive and increasingly insecure. "This is what I wore. I thought it would be okay."

He scrutinized me. "The weight thing needs to come along more quickly, don't you think?"

"But I'm not eating now!" I protested. "I'm starving all the time!"

"You want to look hot on stage, or you want to stuff yourself?" he asked me in a biting voice.

"Well, I want to look hot—"

"Good, then we agree," Trey said, kissing my cheek. All of a sudden he wasn't angry anymore. "You're gonna be unbelievable tonight. I just know it."

"Thanks," I said.

"Knock 'em dead. I'll be right offstage rooting for you."

The manager of the club rounded up the guys, then came and got me. The guys went to their instruments in the dark. I stood in the wings, my legs barely holding me up, while the club manager strode up to the microphone to introduce us.

"Okay, all you party animals," the manager said, "we've got a hot opening act tonight. They've been playing around Nashville, and word is this is a band to watch. Put your hands together for J-J-J-J-Jack Flash!"

The stage lights got brighter, the gels burning

a hot, pulsing red, the band hit the opening licks for their signature song by the Rolling Stones, "Jumpin' Jack Flash," and I ran over to the microphone.

The lights were so bright I couldn't see the crowd. Somehow that made it easier. I closed my eyes and pretended I was in my basement, rocking out, feeling completely comfortable. I turned around at one point, and Ryan gave me a huge grin and a big thumbs-up.

I could do this! I could really, really do this!

When the tune ended, the crowd burst into applause and whistles. It was like a wave of love washing over me. It was the very, very best feeling in the world.

"Thanks very much," I said into the mike, my voice sounding huskier than usual because I'd been rehearsing rock tunes for the past four hours. Sarah Carlton explained to me that rock stars often press down on their vocal cords to get that husky, gravelly sound. She told me you could really damage your chords that way, unless you learned to make the sound correctly.

"I'm Savy Leeman," I told the hushed crowd. I could hear the tremor in my voice. I cleared my throat and took a deep breath. "I'm really happy to be singing for ya'll tonight." I caught Trey's eye off to my right. He was making a "cut" sign at his throat, as in "cut the talking and just sing," but I ignored him and turned back to the crowd. "I'm sitting in for the real lead singer of Jack Flash, Krissy McCaine, who's down with the flu. This next tune is one she wrote, called 'Runnin' Scared.' We hope you like it."

I nodded to the band, and they played the bluesy opening chords of Krissy's song.

Once I lived as your plaything
And you sure kept me in style.
You gave me pearls
And promised the world on a string.
Once I needed protection
From empty arms at midnight.
Till I came upon
A brighter dawn, and I knew
I'd be gone. Now I'm
Runnin' Scared from your love,
Out here on my own. I am
Runnin' Scared from your love,
Got to find my own way back home.
'Cause I have sung your song for much too
long. . . .
Now I'm Runnin' Scared. . . .

It was the strangest thing. As I stood there singing Krissy's song, I suddenly knew it was about her and Trey. And just as suddenly as I knew that, I knew there was more to their story than what Trey had told me.

And I knew I was going to find out.

One last taste of my loving.
One last flame from your fire.
As we kiss and sigh and you tell me lies
One last time.
One man who never loved me.
I see that now in your eyes.
All your alibis,
Your passionate sighs,
Were just lies, I'd despise. . . .
Now I'm Runnin' Scared. . . .

The applause was overwhelming, like nothing I'd ever experienced before. The crowd whistled their approval, stomped their feet, and just kept on clapping.

At that moment it seemed to me that any risk, any lie, was worth this. This magic. This love.

And I never, ever, ever wanted it to end.

Trey and I were in his car, down the block from my house. He had pulled into a dirt turnaround and cut off the ignition. I didn't want him to drive to my house, just in case anyone was still awake.

"You were incredible tonight," he said softly, gently pushing some hair off my face.

"I had the greatest time," I whispered, once again feeling the rush of the applause and the power of the music.

"You are going to go really, really far, little girl," he promised me. He ran one finger down my forehead, down my nose, and over my lips.

I didn't stop to think. I kissed his finger.

The next thing I knew, I was in Trey's arms, and he was kissing me so softly on the lips. I kissed him back, and he held me closer, kissing me like I had never been kissed before, like I'd only ever imagined being kissed.

I felt giddy and weak and dizzy, and I wanted the kiss to go on forever. It was just as good as being onstage.

No, it was maybe even better.

So this is what Kimmy is feeling, I thought. No wonder she's with Sawyer all the time.

"God, Savy," Trey murmured, kissing my neck. I threw my head back and felt the delicious sensation of his lips on my skin.

His mouth headed lower, into the open V of my flowered dress, and I pulled back. "I have to go," I said breathlessly.

"Yeah," he agreed softly, pulling away. "We are an unbelievable team, you know that, don't you?"

"Yeah," I agreed happily. "Good night." I opened the car door, but he pulled me back and kissed me again. And I loved it.

I snuck into the house, my lie already planned out. I would say I had intended to stay over at Kimmy's but had changed my mind.

But when I tiptoed past the kitchen, no one was there.

It was the very first time in my life someone wasn't waiting up for me when I got in.

I breathed a sigh of relief and scurried into my room to call Kimmy. I didn't let myself think about all the lies I was telling or about what had really happened between Krissy and Trey or about Wild Hearts or about school.

Just for that moment I let myself feel perfectly, absolutely, and completely happy.

CHAPTER
10

♡

The next day the proverbial you-know-what hit the fan.

It started out okay. Even though I was operating on a major sleep deficit, I felt good the next morning. I skipped the aerobics class; I figured even Trey would understand, under the circumstances. It was a gorgeous fall day, and the first thing I remembered when I woke up was the feeling of being in Trey's arms. M-mmmmm. Deeeee-licious. Then I remembered the feeling of having all those people applauding and whistling for me after I sang, how I could make people respond, feel things, just by singing. It was so wonderful, and I was so lucky.

Not for long.

I'll remember this moment as long as I live. I went into the breakfast room, and everyone was already there eating except the twins who were who-knows-where and Gramma Beth, who I knew had left very early that morning for a fiddlers' convention in West Virginia.

But everyone else was there—Timmy, Shelly, Mom, and Dad, and they all stared at me when I walked into the room.

"What?" I asked, looking down at myself. I looked normal, I thought, in khaki pleated pants and a white cotton shirt. My pants were looser, I noticed.

No one said anything. My dad just pushed the morning paper, the *Tennessean*, over to the side of the table near where I was standing.

I walked over. It was open to the Living section.

And there on the front page of that section was a photo of me singing with Jack Flash the night before, as well as a photo of Prairie Fire and a review of the concert.

Busted.

"I . . . I . . . I . . ." I stammered. I smiled feebly. "Did I get a good review?" I asked meekly.

No one smiled.

Uh-oh. Humor is the saving grace of my huge,

crazy family. When no one smiles you know you are in deep, deep trouble.

"Clearly you weren't at Kimmy's last night," my mother said in a cold voice.

I sat down in my usual chair at the breakfast table. Shelly's and Timmy's eyes were huge, staring at me.

"No," I admitted.

"You left a note saying you were at Kimmy's," my mom continued, "and you lied to us."

"Yes," I said, gulping hard.

Both my parents heaved a sigh in unison. I felt absolutely terrible.

"Your mother and I need to discuss this," my father finally said. "And we'll talk with you about it this evening. I can say that we are very disappointed in you, Savy."

Tears came to my eyes. Are there any worse words to hear from your parents than "we are very disappointed in you"? Even though I hadn't eaten a thing since the afternoon before, I couldn't put a bite in my mouth. Well, misery was one way to lose weight.

The day went downhill from there. I walked into school and saw Kimmy, Jane, and Sandra huddled together in the hall. They all turned and looked at me, their eyes hard and cold.

And I knew they knew.

"It's not what you think" was the first thing I said to them.

Kimmy looked ready to cry. "You used me. You had me cover for you so you could go be in someone else's band!"

"No, no, I'm not in their band!" I protested. "I just filled in because their lead singer was sick!"

"You know, somehow I just don't buy that," Sandra said in measured tones. "You've been acting really strange lately. You haven't even wanted to have band practice."

"This is uncool in a major way," Jane added, looking at me with disgust. "You, like, lied to all of us!"

"How could you?" Kimmy yelled.

"But I didn't leave Wild Hearts, I swear!" I cried. "What happened is that—"

"Savy, the truth is right here, so don't give us that," Jane said, brandishing the Living section of the *Tennessean* in my face.

"But if you would just let me explain—" I began.

"I don't want to hear it," Sandra said, cutting me off. She took the *Tennessean* from Jane and dropped it on top of the schoolbooks in her arms. "Frankly, right now I just want you out of my face." Then she turned around and stomped off.

Jane shook her head at me and followed Sandra, and finally even Kimmy, my best friend in the world, turned away.

The bell for first period rang, but I just ignored it. I ran to the girls' room and locked myself in the stall, and then I cried like my heart was breaking, which was exactly how it felt.

"Savy, could I speak with you, please?" Ms. Millman said to me after class. I trudged over to her desk.

"How do you think you did on the quiz today?" she asked me.

"I think I flunked it," I said bluntly, tears springing to my eyes. I was so screwed. All my plans for studying extra hard so I would ace that quiz had disappeared in my excitement over singing with Jack Flash the night before.

Ms. Millman sighed. "Have you asked your parents to come in to speak with me?"

"No," I replied. Frankly I was sick of lying.

"May I ask why?"

"Because they'll kill me," I replied.

Ms. Millman tapped her finger on her desk as she thought. "You know, I'm perfectly aware of how intelligent you are, Savy. And I'm also aware that you don't have much interest in American history." She allowed herself a little smile. "But . . . I feel as if something is troubling you, which troubles me. Do you want to talk about it?"

I shook my head no. If I opened my mouth, I was sure I would just burst out sobbing. Besides, I didn't feel particularly close to Ms. Millman. She wasn't someone I'd want to spill my guts to.

She sighed again. "Well, there's only one thing I can think of to do, then. I'm going to insist that you speak with your parents today, and I will call them this evening to make sure you've done so."

Great. Just great. Why didn't I just dig a hole, crawl in, and die?

I trudged out of history class, everything a blur from the tears in my eyes.

"Hey, Savy, congrats!" Betsy Winters called to me from across the hall. She's a girl I've gone to school with for years, very brainy, very nice. She ran over to me.

I quickly brushed the tears out of my eyes, but she saw them anyway.

"Are you okay?"

"Yeah, I just have a cold," I improvised. "What's up?"

"I read that review about you in the *Tennessean*," Betsy said. "Pretty nice, huh?"

"Is it?" I asked dully.

She looked at me like I was crazy. "Are you kidding? The reviewer said you sounded like Patsy Cline! How much better than that can you get?"

"Yeah," I agreed listlessly. So I had gotten a good review. I still hadn't read the article. But what difference did it make, anyway? Everyone who counted hated me.

"I heard Jack Flash a few months ago at a party," Betsy continued eagerly. "They were great. Wow, it was such a cool break for you, don't you think? Their lead singer getting the flu and you getting to fill in? How did they even know about you, anyway?"

I stared at Betsy. "What did you say?"

"I said how did they know about you?"

"No, no, the part about the flu," I insisted, grabbing her arm hard.

"I read it in the review," Betsy said, giving me a strange look. "Are you sure you're okay?"

A grin spread across my face. "I am very okay. More than okay. Thanks, Betsy!" I ran to the stairwell and sat down on the top step. Then I pulled the *Tennessean* out from my notebook and eagerly read the review.

ROCK THE HOUSE—TWO TO WATCH
by Michael Zimmerman

Last night at the Big Bamboo the crowd was treated to a first-rate night of rock by two hot Nashville bands, Jack Flash and Prairie Fire. Prairie Fire recently signed a deal with

RCA, and if last night was any indication, Jack Flash will soon follow suit.

Opening with a mixed set of originals and classic covers, Jack Flash was fronted by stand-in lead singer Savy Leeman, covering for Krissy McCaine, out with the flu. Savy Leeman lacks the been-around-the-block growl to her voice that Krissy has, but her smooth, heartfelt powerhouse voice reminded me of a soulful Patsy Cline. In a town full of singers, she is definitely one to watch. . . .

Yes! Here was the truth, in black and white! The fact that the reviewer had loved my voice was not foremost in my mind; the fact that here was proof that I hadn't joined another band behind my friends' backs was.

I ran to the lunchroom and found my three best friends—at least I hoped they still were— sitting at our usual spot. I plopped down next to Kimmy and threw the *Tennessean* on the table.

"Read," I commanded.

"What for?" Jane asked sourly.

"Okay, I'll read it," I said, picking up the paper. And then I read them the part that said I was covering for Krissy, who was out with the flu.

They all looked at me.

"So ... you really didn't join another band?" Kimmy asked timidly.

"That's what I tried to tell ya'll!" I cried.

"We never actually read the review," Kimmy acknowledged.

"Obviously," I agreed. "I was just filling in! Trey called me in the afternoon, and he was desperate."

"So why didn't you just tell us that?" Sandra asked me.

"I should have," I admitted.

"And who the hell is Trey?" Jane asked, stirring the fruit up from the bottom of her yogurt.

"My manager," I blurted out. "I mean ... Well, he's a guy who kind of wants to manage my singing career. And he manages Jack Flash, too."

"Excuse me, but did I miss something?" Jane asked. "I thought we were a band. How could you have a manager for your 'singing career' when this Trey guy doesn't manage the band?"

"Well, um ..." I stammered. I couldn't figure out how to explain it. It had seemed to make so much sense to me at the time. I remembered my grandmother telling me that I needed to discuss this with the rest of the band. Well, I hadn't. Dumb move.

"He's just helping me to have a better sound and stuff," I said lamely. I sounded ridiculous, even to my own ears.

"Yeah, so what's in it for him?" the ever-practical Sandra asked me.

"Well, a percentage of my income when I start making money," I explained.

"Your income, or Wild Hearts' income?" Sandra asked.

"Mine, I guess," I replied lamely.

"Oh, so this dude is gonna get fifteen percent of your twenty-five percent of what Wild Hearts gets, is that it?" Sandra demanded.

I hadn't thought about it that way. "Look, I didn't sign anything—"

"It sounds like you didn't *think* about anything, either," Sandra said bluntly. She crumpled her brown paper bag and tossed it across to the wastepaper basket, a perfect shot.

"Look, Wild Hearts means everything to me," I told them. "That hasn't changed."

Sandra gave me a long look. "I was just telling Kimmy and Jane," she said. "Wild Hearts has been invited to play at the Multicultural Festival downtown this Saturday. A woman on their board heard us play at the arthritis telethon. We'd do two sets, from nine until eleven."

"That's great!" I said eagerly.

"Yeah," Jane agreed, "except we haven't even practiced in a long time. I thought you cared about our band being excellent?"

"I do!" I insisted.

"Well, you haven't been acting like it," Jane said.

"So we'll practice between now and Saturday," I said. "A lot. Okay?"

They all looked at each other.

"Can we have a practice tonight, say, tonight after dinner?" Sandra asked.

My voice lesson had been switched to tonight after dinner. Well, I'd just have to cancel it. "Of course," I said. "Ya'll in?"

Everyone nodded, even Kimmy. And she didn't say a word about our looking for another guitar player.

"Well, okay," Sandra said. "I'll tell this woman yes for Saturday." She got up from the bench.

I got up, too. "We're gonna be great, you'll see," I told Sandra, gathering up my books. "So how about if we meet at my house tonight at, say, seven?"

Everyone agreed, and we all went our separate ways. Kimmy ran over to Sawyer, and Jane and Sandra headed off together.

Well, there was still hope that I hadn't ruined everything.

Unless, of course, my parents grounded me. And said I couldn't have band practice. Or even play in the band.

But no, they'd never do that. They were musicians. They knew what music meant to me.

Then I remembered. I had to tell them I was flunking history, and they had to come in and see Ms. Millman.

They weren't just going to ground me. They were going to kill me.

CHAPTER
11

♡

Nice place," Trey said, stepping into the front hall of my house.

It was early evening. Trey had called me right after school and said he needed to meet with me about something really exciting, so I'd invited him over. I figured I'd better be around whenever my parents showed up for our Big Talk, or I'd be in even more trouble than I was already.

As if that was possible.

Trey wrapped his arms around me and kissed me. Fortunately no one was around at the moment. I buried my face in his fragrant neck and immediately felt better. He was so cute, so fabulous, and he really cared about me.

He stepped back and looked around. Our house is very large, but as I said, it's in a constant state of makeover-in-progress. I watched Trey as he took in the different wallpapers in the living room, the fabric samples in the dining room, and the half refinished cabinets in the kitchen that were partly visible from the hall.

"Are you redoing the interior?" Trey asked curiously.

"Constantly," I replied, and led him by the hand into the living room. We sat next to each other on the couch, holding hands.

"Did I mention how fabulous you were last night?" Trey asked me, leaning over to kiss me again.

"Once or twice," I said with a grin.

"You really came through for me, babe. That means a lot."

"You're welcome," I said happily. "It was so exciting—it was . . . it's so hard to describe—"

"Like it's where you're supposed to be and what you're supposed to be doing, right?" Trey asked softly.

"Yes, that's it!" I agreed eagerly. "I never wanted it to end!"

"It doesn't have to," Trey said softly, lifting a few strands of hair off my neck. "After that review you got, the sky is the limit."

When Trey mentioned the review, it reminded me of how much trouble I was in. I shifted my weight away from him. "So what did you want to talk with me about?"

Trey's eyes lit up with excitement. "I got a call this morning from none other than Lemont Cantrell's assistant at Avalon Records."

"Who's that?" I asked.

"Lemont Cantrell used to be head of Megaphonics, the biggest label in Nashville," Trey explained. "He just left to start his own label, Avalon. Anyway, the word is that he's looking for hot young crossover artists—country to pop rock. Well, Lemont's assistant, Pam Sterling, was at the Big Bamboo last night, and she heard you sing. She was blown away, Savy. Seriously blown away."

"Really?" I asked eagerly.

"Really," Trey confirmed. "Anyway, Pam told Lemont about you, and she showed him the review in the *Tennessean,* and he wants to hear you sing!"

"No way!" I cried.

Trey just grinned and leaned over to give me a quick kiss. "Savy, this is really, really big! Avalon is the perfect place for us! This guy can really make it happen for both of us! I'm not kidding!"

My heart was beating so fast I could hardly

breathe. Everything was happening so fast! It was wonderful, unbelievable ... and really, really scary.

"So ... so what do we do now?" I asked Trey.

"He wants you to showcase at Derek's Corner on Saturday night so he can come watch you work," Trey said. "Figure on doing, say, six tunes. Jack Flash will back you up. I already called and arranged it with the guys in the band and with the club."

Saturday night. I had promised to play with Wild Hearts on Saturday night. If I canceled, it would be the end of the band. But how could I possibly turn down this opportunity?

"What time would I go on?" I asked Trey carefully.

"You're booked for eleven." He scrutinized my face. "Hey, you don't look very happy for a kid who just got the break of a lifetime."

"No, I'm happy," I assured him. "I'm really happy. I just . . . I have to make some arrangements."

I calculated quickly. The party where Wild Hearts was playing was supposed to end at eleven. If I ducked out a little early, I could make it over to Derek's Corner just in time to sing with Jack Flash. It was doable.

"What about Krissy?" I asked carefully. "Jack Flash is still her band."

"Not anymore," Trey said in a hard voice. "She finally got her butt into a rehab program, according to a message some guy left on my machine. She's at some place called Manor House trying to get straight. It's about an hour outside Nashville. The guy on the phone, who didn't even bother to identify himself, said she'd be there for at least sixty days. Then she's going home to Memphis for a while to chill—whatever that means."

"Well, that's good," I said. "She needs help."

"Hey, good riddance to your basic bad rubbish," Trey snorted. "I did everything for Krissy, but she just couldn't cut it. The dude who called me is probably her new squeeze—that jerk in the red Miata who whisked her off from the gig yesterday." He reached over and took my hand. "Hey, forget about her. Let's talk about you. We've got a lot of work to do between now and Saturday, right?"

"Right," I agreed.

"Okay, first thing is this—don't get freaked out. Pam told me on the phone that when Lemont saw your photo in the paper he said, 'She's kind of a plump little thing, isn't she?'"

"But I've lost five pounds!" I protested. "I just have a round face."

"Honey, baby fat will never make you a star,"

Trey said slowly, as if I were stupid as well as chubby. "Baby fat doesn't photograph. Baby fat doesn't make guys want you. Baby fat means no record deal. Now, you want to blow this chance?"

"No, of course not," I replied, "but I'm doing everything I can do—"

Trey reached into his pocket and took out a small vial of red capsules. "This would help do the trick, you know," he said. He opened the vial and took out a pill, holding it in the palm of his hand.

"What is it?" I asked warily.

"It's perfectly natural," he said. "It kills your appetite and gives you tons of energy."

"It's speed," I said, "and it's not perfectly natural. And no, thanks."

He took my hand and put the pill in my palm, then curled my fingers around it. "Don't take it if you don't want to," he told me. "But this diet thing is going pretty slow, and you seem to be slowing down. I heard you weren't at your aerobics class this morning."

My mouth dropped open. "You checked up on me?"

Trey gave me a loving smile. "It's my job, sweetie. Now, aren't you glad I care that much about you?"

"Well, yes," I allowed, "but—"

"Shh," he crooned, and dropped the vial of pills into the pocket of my shirt. "I am the manager, and you are the talent. I know what I'm doing, Savy. You trust me, right?"

"Right," I said hesitantly. "But—"

"Look, either you do or you don't," Trey interrupted me. "Or are you gonna be just like Krissy, someone who can't take the heat?"

"No, I'm—"

"Because if that's the deal, tell me now," Trey said, standing up. His voice sounded hard and cold, but then his face changed as sorrow flitted across his brow. He took a deep breath. "You don't believe in me. I see it in your eyes."

"It isn't that," I insisted.

"You don't know much about me," Trey said. "Well, not many people do. But . . . I care about you, Savy. So . . ." he let the rest of his sentence dangle in the air. "I come from that little town Dickson, you know, the one outside Nashville that everyone jokes about because it's supposed to be so poor?"

I nodded.

"Yeah, well, we were even poorer than that. I'm not telling you this so you'll feel sorry for me," Trey said. "I'm just trying to explain. No one in my family ever went to college, but everyone made music—"

"Like my family," I interrupted.

"Right," he agreed. "Except that my family didn't have a pot to piss in. Anyway, I always knew that if my parents had just had someone to manage their talent, they could have been big stars. But they never did. So I vowed that's what I was going to learn to do. I got a full scholarship to Vanderbilt, and I started managing bands when I was just a freshman. But by then it was too late for my parents. My mom died from cancer, and my dad drank himself to death."

"Oh, Trey ..." I said softly, touching his shoulder.

He grabbed my hand. "Look, this is not some big sob story. I lost my chance with them, and then I spent the next three years looking for someone with the right combination of talent and looks and drive, and I found Krissy. Well, you know what happened. And now there's you. I just can't have my heart broken again, you know what I mean?"

"I know," I said fervently. I stood up quickly and put my arms around him. "You can count on me, I promise. I won't disappoint you!"

Trey put his arms around me and held me close; then he gave me the softest, sweetest kiss in the world. "I only want what's best for you, Savy," he said earnestly. "If a little thing like a few pounds is gonna keep you from success, then I've got to tell you, don't I?"

"I guess so," I answered.

"You've got the voice. Now you need the look. You take off at least three, four more pounds before Saturday, and we'll go shopping together for your stage outfit for the big night, okay?"

"Okay," I agreed hesitantly, because some part of me didn't agree at all.

Trey tipped my chin up so that he could look directly into my eyes. "And you know I'll know, sweetheart, because I'll have you weighed in at the gym. And I'll know if you miss an aerobics class again, too. If you don't follow the program, the whole deal is off. I'm only doing this for your own good. Are you with me?"

I nodded yes.

"Oh, and one last thing. Lemont Cantrell thinks you're twenty-two. Let's keep it that way, okay? No way is he gonna mess with a sixteen-year-old kid."

I reluctantly nodded again.

Trey grinned. "Hey, what can I say, you've got talent and maturity beyond your tender years," he said in a teasing voice. Then he turned serious. "When opportunity comes knockin' at your door, Savy, you've got to seize the moment, because it may never knock again."

I found myself nodding once more.

"That's my girl," Trey said, and he cupped my face in his hands and gave me a long, slow, sizzling kiss.

"Oooooooo! I saw!" Timmy screeched from the doorway.

Trey and I both turned to look. There was my little brother, Timmy, and my little sister, Shelly, falling all over each other in a fit of giggles.

"Is he your boyfriend?" Shelly asked, wide-eyed, when she could stop laughing.

I looked at Trey. I didn't know what to say.

"Absolutely," Trey said firmly, putting his arm around my waist. "I am absolutely her guy. And she's my girl."

I felt like throwing up.

An hour after Trey left, I was sitting in the exact same room with my mother and father while they lowered the boom on my entire life. Before they could even begin to light into me about what I'd done the night before, I had to tell them about how I was flunking history and how Ms. Millman insisted they come to school.

And if all that wasn't bad enough, in just a half hour Kimmy, Sandra, and Jane were due to show up for band practice.

Which my parents knew nothing about.

"You know, in addition to feeling angry with you, we feel hurt," my mother said. "And confused. And concerned."

I gulped hard. It would be easier if they could just be pissed off, punish me, the end.

"We have such trust in you," my father said, taking up where my mother had left off. "And up until now you've never given us any reason *not* to trust you."

A tear slid out of the corner of my eye. I quickly brushed it away with the back of my hand.

"Maybe we haven't been paying as much attention to you as we should," my mother mused. "We've been so concerned about . . ." My father caught her eye, and it seemed to me that something she saw in his expression told her not to finish her sentence. "Anyway," she continued, "we want to know why you lied to us and what's going on."

So I told them about Trey and how much he believed in my talent and how he was helping me with my career.

My father gave me a sharp look. "Are you involved with this boy?"

"Involved how?" I hedged.

"We saw them kissing!" Timmy yelled from the doorway.

I wanted to throttle him.

"Timmy, please go to your room. This is private," my father told him sternly. He turned back to me. "Well?"

"Well, yes, I'm involved with him," I admitted.

"And just how old is this fellow?" my father probed.

Gulp. "Uh, twenty-two," I mumbled.

"Twenty-two?" my father roared. "Did you say *twenty-two?"*

"Don't yell, honey. She can hear you," my mother said softly.

I could see my father fighting for self-control. "Did you say he is twenty-two years old?" my father asked me in a barely controlled voice.

"Yes," I admitted. "But age isn't relevant here, Daddy—"

"When my sixteen-year-old *underage* daughter is sneaking out to go to a bar with a twenty-two-year-old man, age most certainly is relevant! You have no business being with him at all—much less at a bar!"

"You see, that's why I couldn't tell you the truth!" I cried. "I wasn't going to a bar to drink. I was going there to sing!"

"Look, let's put your relationship with this boy aside for a moment," my mother said, patting my father's hand to calm him down. "If you lie to us, we can't trust you; it's as simple as that."

"I know," I said in a defeated voice.

"And this whole thing with school," my mother continued, "flunking history ... it's just not like you! Is something troubling you?"

"No," I said. "It's just that music is so much more important to me than American history!"

"We know that," my mother said. "You don't have to like history, but you do have to study and do reasonably well."

"Like make the honor roll," my father put in, "instead of sneaking out to bars with—"

"Hush," my mother said. She turned to me. "Well, Savy, we have to punish you for lying and for not studying. You know that."

I nodded morosely.

"You will be grounded for two weeks, from everything except Wild Hearts," my father said in a stern voice. "Your mama and I have discussed it, and we've decided to let you continue with your band because we know how much it means to you and we want to encourage your talent."

"Oh, thank you, Daddy. I—"

"Wait a minute, I'm not through," my father said, holding his palm up in the air. "There's more. This whole thing with your history grade is a new wrinkle. We will go in and see your history teacher. In turn, you will get no less than a B on every quiz and test in history class—in fact, in *all* your classes—or we will pull you out of your band."

"I understand," I agreed readily, so happy to hear I could continue my music.

"And," my father continued, "you will stop seeing this Trey person, both personally and professionally."

I stared at my father. "But ... but I can't—"

"We know you don't want to stop seeing him, honey," my mother said. "But we have to insist."

"But you don't even know him!" I protested. "He's a terrific guy—"

"He's too old for you," my father said bluntly.

"But that's not fair!" I looked at my father. "You're six years older than Mom, so what does age have to do with anything?"

"It has a lot to do with you sneaking out and going to a bar, evidently," my father said dryly.

I jumped up from the couch. "What if Dustin was dating a sixteen-year-old girl?" I asked. "Would you insist that he stop seeing her?"

"That's different," my father said.

"Because he's a guy?" I sneered.

"You know that isn't why," my mother said. "It's because he's not sixteen, and you are."

"But Trey already got me an audition with the head of Avalon Records—"

"Does the head of Avalon Records know you're only sixteen?" my father asked.

"Well, no," I admitted, "but what difference would that make?"

"The difference that would make is that you are not allowed in places where they serve alcohol," my mother said patiently. "And you can't sign contracts. And you can't tour. All of which would make it pretty tough for him to make any money off you right now."

"So what am I supposed to do, turn down the biggest opportunity I've ever had because I'm sixteen?" I exploded.

"If this—what's his name?" my father asked.

"Lemont Cantrell," I filled in. "He's famous."

"Yeah, I've heard of him," my father allowed. "But if this man is interested in you now, he'll still be interested in you when you're eighteen, at which time you can make your own decision about your future."

"But that's two years from now!" I cried. "That's like . . . forever!"

"It just seems like forever," my mother said. "What we really want you to do is go to college— that's no news to you—but if you decide to pursue a career as a professional performer at that time, we won't stand in your way."

"Although it would kill your grandmother," my father put in tersely.

"That's not true," I said fervently. "Gramma Beth understands me better than you do."

My parents shared that strange look again.

"You'll have plenty of opportunities to sing for people like Cantrell," my father said. "Don't be in such a rush."

Seize the day, Trey had said. But my parents just didn't understand. Maybe I'd never have another chance to sing for Lemont Cantrell. Maybe two years from now he'd have all the young female singers he needed. Maybe this was meant to be my one big chance. How could I possibly let it pass me by just because I had the bad luck to be only sixteen years old?

I slumped back down on the couch, defeated. As I sat back down, my khaki pants, now big on me, slid with me until they were a couple of inches below my waist. I hiked them up.

"You're losing weight," my mother said, a note of concern in her voice.

"I'm dieting," I explained. I remembered that the vial of red pills was still in my pocket. My God, if my parents saw those, I'd be locked in my room for the rest of my life.

"You don't need to diet," my father said. "Are you doing it for this Trey person?"

"His name is Trey Jackson," I said with dignity. "And I'm not dieting for him."

"Well, please take care of yourself," my mother said. "And don't lose any more weight. You really don't need to."

I looked at my watch. "The band is due here in fifteen minutes for rehearsal," I said, wanting to get off the subject of my weight. "I didn't have time to tell you before."

"All right," my mother said. "But you understand everything we've laid out here? We're very serious about this, Savy."

"I understand," I said.

"Good," my mother said. "Because if you don't follow the rules, you're out of Wild Hearts. Permanently."

CHAPTER
12

Savy, are you okay?" Kimmy asked me.

"Huh, what?" I asked her.

"Are you sick or something?"

It was two evenings later, and I felt like jumping out of my skin, I was so hyper.

But it wasn't my fault. That's what I told myself.

I had dutifully gotten up every morning and killed myself at that stupid aerobics class. Then I'd gone to school and actually paid attention in every class. Then I had come home and studied like a maniac. Then I either had a Wild Hearts practice, a voice lesson, or a session with Trey to work on material.

And I was doing all of this without eating.

I had bought a supply of this liquid diet stuff I'd seen advertised on television—it's called Super-Loss. It was supposed to taste like a milk shake. It didn't. And it was supposed to provide all the vitamins and nutrients I would need to get through the day, as long as I ate a "balanced dinner." Well, I was pretty generally skipping dinner, and I was so exhausted and so hungry that I thought about food all the time.

That is, when I could keep my eyes open.

But ... I had lost two more pounds. And I'd gotten a B-plus on my history quiz. And my friends were speaking to me again.

But that morning when the alarm went off for the aerobics class, I couldn't even get out of bed. Every bone in my body hurt. I was so exhausted and so hungry I could hardly move. But I had to. Trey would know if I skipped the class. And if I missed even a day of school, my grades might slip back. There was just too much at stake.

It was then that I remembered the little red pill.

I knew—and still know, for that matter—a lot of kids who did drugs. From pot to coke to pills, drugs are easy to get and, generally speaking, easy to hide from parents. I have never been interested, myself. In fact, I think drugs are a stupid

waste of time, totally lame. It isn't a moral thing
with me; I've just never known drugs to do anything good for anybody. It's kind of like alcohol—you think you're being very cool, when the
truth is, you're making a total weenie out of
yourself.

But. Somehow as I lay there in bed, so tired
and so hungry and so totally stressed out about
my life, I forgot all of that. And I remembered
that the little red pill was supposed to give me
lots of energy and cut my appetite.

That was exactly what I needed.

I got up and found my white shirt hanging in
the closet, the vial of pills in the pocket. Before
I could allow myself to think too much about it, I
dropped one into my palm, ran to the bathroom,
popped it, and drank some water.

It wasn't long before I got a huge rush of energy. My hunger faded like a bad dream. Yes!
This was going to work!

As I quickly dressed for the aerobics class, I
thought about Trey. I hadn't broken up with him,
either personally or professionally. But I felt totally self-righteous about lying to my parents
now. How dare they think they had the right to
tell me what guy I could like? How dare they
condemn him when they'd never even met him?
It was so hypocritical, and I was so angry, that I

rationalized that I had the right to see him behind their backs.

Maybe they still thought of me as their little girl, but I wasn't. And that was that.

Trey still wanted me to lose two more pounds before Saturday. In fact, he insisted. I couldn't blame him. This was such a big opportunity for both of us. What if I blew it with Lemont Cantrell just because he thought I looked too fat?

I buzzed through the aerobics class, and the day at school just flew by. I didn't bother with the Super-Loss at lunch—why should I? I didn't have any appetite. When I got home, I studied. Then I went out jogging while my family ate dinner; I told them I had eaten at a nearby friend's house while I was out. After that I had Wild Hearts rehearsal, and now that practice had ended and Jane and Sandra had gone home, Kimmy and I were hanging out. I was glad, because it seemed like forever since the two of us had just chilled together. No guys, no band, just us.

The only problem was, the little red pill was wearing off. No, it had worn off. And I felt like roadkill.

"I'm not sick," I told her. "I'm just a little tired."

She narrowed her eyes at me. "I don't think you look very good."

I jumped up from the couch where we were sitting. "I look great!" I said, sticking my hand into the waistband of my jeans. "Look how big these are on me!"

"From drinking that junk at lunchtime?" Kimmy asked dubiously.

My friends had seen me chugging down my Super-Loss at lunchtime. I told them I was eating the other meals, so they wouldn't rag on me. How could they possibly understand? Kimmy was naturally skinny, Jane was the perfect weight for her height, and Sandra had the perfectly aerobicized body of a jock. A record executive would never turn any of them down because of baby fat.

"It's not junk," I replied, plopping back down on the couch. "Besides, Trey likes me this way."

Kimmy cocked her head to one side. "Is he . . . you know . . . *it*?"

"It?"

"The love of your life?" Kimmy translated eagerly.

"How would I know?" I asked irritably. My stomach made growling noises. I could still smell the delicious aroma of the roast duck Magenta Sue had made for dinner. The roast duck I hadn't eaten. In fact, now that I thought about it, I hadn't eaten all day.

"If he was, you'd know," Kimmy said sagely.

"Oh, come on, Kimmy," I scoffed.

"No, it's true," she insisted.

"How could you possibly know?" I asked her. "Sawyer is the first guy you ever even *kissed*!"

"I just know."

"That is stupid," I snapped.

Silence.

"I'm sorry," I said finally. "I'm being a witch. I'm just ... I've got a lot on my mind." I was so hungry I could have eaten the half-reupholstered couch. I either had to eat or take another pill. And I knew if I ate, it wasn't going to be a small salad with no dressing; it was going to be everything in the refrigerator. And then my diet would be blown. And then I'd weigh in higher tomorrow, and then Trey would know. And then ...

"Savy?" Kimmy whispered.

"What?"

"What's on your mind? I mean, do you want to talk about it?"

"It's no big thing," I insisted, sloughing off her concern. "Just, you know, the usual stuff."

Kimmy had her glasses on, and her eyes looked huge and worried behind the lenses. She tentatively touched my arm. "I feel ... funny. Like you won't talk to me. Like something is going on and you won't tell me."

"No, nothing," I insisted.

"But—"

"But what?" I interrupted her. "Look, things are changing. You're the one who told me that. You have Sawyer now. And I have Trey. We're not two kids who tell each other every little thing anymore!"

She looked so sad. One part of me wanted to comfort her. I had spent so many years making sure Kimmy was okay. Well, those days were over. She didn't need me anymore. And she wasn't my responsibility.

"Maybe the four of us could double-date sometime," she suggested shyly.

"Maybe," I said vaguely.

And then I thought about that. I had never actually gone out on a date with Trey. We were always working on music. Sure, he kissed me and said sweet things to me, but we had never done so much as see a movie together.

There was an awkward silence in the room. It was so weird. I couldn't remember ever, ever feeling awkward with Kimmy.

"Hey, you know what Sawyer said?" Kimmy asked a little too eagerly. "I was talking with him about Wild Hearts, and he said he thinks I should stay in the band."

That got my attention. "And?" I asked.

"And ... I'm thinking about it."

"Hold the phone," I said. "Are you saying that Sawyer opens his little ole mouth and mentions that maybe you should stay in the band, and that makes you think about it, but when I, supposedly your best friend, beg and plead with you to stay in the band, you turn me down flat? Is that what you're saying?" My voice was rising uncontrollably.

"But ... but it's not like that, Savy!" Kimmy insisted with alarm.

"No? How is it, then," I shot back, folding my arms.

Kimmy's face blazed a bright red. "I ... I feel so terrible about Sawyer getting shot because of me. I mean, I feel responsible. I owe it to him to consider how he feels about this!"

"Oh, that's bull!" I sneered. "You're just turning into one of the Pastel People. Sawyer says 'Jump,' and you say 'How high?' "

"But I thought you'd be happy!" Kimmy exclaimed. "I thought you'd be glad to hear that I'm thinking about staying in the band!"

"Don't do me any favors."

Kimmy stared at me a moment and then buried her head in her hands. "Oh, God—"

"Stop it! Just stop it!" I yelled, jumping up. "I don't want to comfort you and make you feel better, Kimmy! I've got my own problems!"

She stood up, too. "But I never asked you to—"

"I'm not doing what everyone expects me to do anymore! I'm doing what I want to do!"

"But—"

"I gotta go, Kimmy. Just . . . I gotta go."

I flew out of the music room, leaving her there in the basement with that horrible, hurt, bewildered look on her face. I ran up to my room and slammed the door, determined to get out my schoolbooks, forget about Kimmy and food and the little red pills that were in my desk drawer, hidden under some scarves. I could do it. All it took was willpower.

But I was so hungry I couldn't think.

And the little red pills were calling to me.

CHAPTER
13

♡

"How about this, babe?" Trey asked me, holding up a hot pink dress made of some kind of stretchy material. It was about the size of a small child's T-shirt.

It was Saturday afternoon, and we were at the Green Hills Mall, shopping for my outfit for that night. I had only popped half of a little red pill, because it scared me so much that I was taking them so often. In fact, I only had two left. I was much thinner, but I felt awful. I wasn't sleeping, and I felt anxious, irritable, on edge.

"Isn't that dress a little skimpy?" I asked him.

Trey kissed my cheek. "On the old you, maybe," he allowed. "Who would've wanted to look at all that pudge? But, sweetie, you are only five or so pounds from perfection. This would look great on you!"

Five or so pounds from perfection? I could feel my hipbones jutting out. My parents had told me that if they didn't see me eating, they would start to force-feed me. I knew Gramma Beth was going to have a fit when she got back from the fiddlers' convention.

"Just go try it on," Trey coaxed. "For me."

Reluctantly I took the dress and went off to the dressing room. I pulled off my jeans and T-shirt and caught a glimpse of myself in the mirror just before I pulled the pink dress over my head.

I looked awful. There were dark circles under my eyes. My naturally curly red hair looked limp and dry. I stuck my tongue out at myself. I just needed to get some rest, that was all. That's what I told myself. Then I slid into the dress and went out so Trey could see me.

"Wow, it's fabulous!" he cried.

I tugged at the bottom of the dress, which ended somewhere just below a point at which I could probably get arrested. "But ... it doesn't feel like me," I explained.

"That's the old you!" Trey insisted. "Forget that chubbed-out girl-next-door thing, babe!"

Is that how he had thought of me, as a chubbed-out girl-next-door?

"Now let's think about the shoes," Trey mused, as if we'd both already decided on this dress. "I think really high heels, don't you? Since you're so short?"

"But I hate heels!" I protested. "I can't even walk across a room in high heels!"

"You'll learn," Trey said distractedly, looking around for the shoe section of the store.

"No," I told him adamantly. "No heels. They're not even hip anymore."

Trey sighed and shook his head. "Okay, let's go over it again. Tonight you need to impress a middle-aged man. A middle-aged man who can make or break it for us. Now, middle-aged guys like high heels. You are short. Your legs are short. You will look stocky if you don't wear heels."

Stocky?

"Well, maybe just a little heel . . ." I demurred.

"Cool," Trey said, giving me a bear hug. "So go change out of the dress, and we'll find you some hot pumps."

I dutifully changed out of the dress, my stomach rumbling all the while. Half of a red didn't begin to do what a whole red did. Like completely kill my appetite, for example.

We found some pink suede heels that Trey loved and I hated, but I was just too tired to put up an argument. Then he drove me to Kimmy's.

I had an overnight bag full of my stuff in his car. I had told my parents I was going to dress for my gig with Wild Hearts at Kimmy's. Then my plan was to leave the Multicultural Festival, taxi over to Derek's Corner, run into the dressing room and change, and then sing with Jack Flash for Lemont Cantrell.

Kimmy and I had made up, but things still weren't right between us. Too much left unsaid. Too many changes.

"Your friend Kimmy actually lives here?" Trey asked as he pulled into her circular driveway after being cleared by the guard. "This is the biggest house I ever saw."

"She hates it," I told him. "She's not a snob or anything."

Trey smiled ruefully. "Now, why is it that poor people never have to worry about people taking them to be a snob?" He kissed me lightly. "So, I'll see you at Derek's Corner at, say, ten-thirty?"

"Sure," I agreed, even though I knew I couldn't possibly make it there by ten-thirty. But I didn't want to tell Trey I was singing with Wild Hearts first. He would just make a scene about what a waste of time that was, and he'd try to browbeat me into leaving my band. So I didn't tell him.

It will all work out, I chanted to myself as I

knocked on Kimmy's front door and Trey sped off in his car. It will all work out. I can make it work out.

"Hi," Kimmy said, answering the door herself. She peered out after Trey's car. "Why didn't you invite him in? I wanted to meet him."

"He was in a hurry," I invented, walking into the huge front hallway.

"We just sat down to eat," Kimmy explained to me. "Come on in."

"Oh, I'm not hungry," I said quickly.

"Kimberly?" Kimmy's mother called from the dining room. "Please bring Savannah in here."

Kimmy rolled her eyes. "Her Majesty requests your presence," she whispered to me.

We walked into the dining room where Kimmy's mother sat at the end of a huge formal table laden with silver chafing dishes.

"Hello, Savannah," Mrs. Carrier said in her genteel southern tones. "How nice to see you."

She didn't mean this, of course. She isn't fond of me. I think Kimmy's mother is anti-Semitic actually. But it just wouldn't be good breeding to admit it.

"Nice to see you, too, Mrs. Carrier," I said politely.

"Do sit down," she said, cocking her head toward an oversized tapestry-backed chair. "You too, Kimberly."

We sat.

Then a maid wearing an actual maid's uniform came in and offered a platter of roast beef to each of us in turn.

"You're looking thinner, Savannah," Mrs. Carrier said, helping herself to some of the roast beef. "It's very becoming."

"Thanks," I said, my mouth watering so much at the sight of all that food that I was afraid I'd start to drool on the table at any minute. I took a slice of the roast beef when it was offered to me. And I took mashed potatoes. And glazed carrots. And tiny fragrant rolls with chive butter.

I planned to just mush the food all around on my plate so it would look as if I had eaten something.

Mrs. Carrier began to tell some story about something or other that had happened with her charitable foundation, but I couldn't hear a thing. All I could think about was that food. That food. That food that I couldn't eat.

I had to take another red. I had to.

"Excuse me," I blurted out, and jumped up from the table. I grabbed my purse and ran to the bathroom. Then I sat on the edge of the tub and rummaged around until I found the vial of pills. Only two were left.

I popped both of them and slurped some water

into my mouth. Then I took a few deep breaths and headed back to the dining room.

In control.

"Ladies and gentlemen, please give a warm welcome to our next band, Wild Hearts!"

Two outdoor stages had been set up downtown for the Multicultural Festival. The night would be devoted to bands of all types. While a reggae band was performing on one stage, we set up our equipment on the other. The weather was terrible, and the entertainment was running an hour behind schedule because it had been pouring earlier. Now the rain had slowed down, but not very many people had stayed at the festival. The MC—she never told us who she was—seemed discouraged and depressed, and who could blame her? Her festival was getting rained out.

Still, I was totally revved. The two reds I had taken were coursing through my bloodstream. I felt like I was on top of the world.

We opened with "Great Balls of Fire," an old Jerry Lee Lewis tune that we do really well. It's a rocker that gets everyone's attention. Sawyer was standing down front staring up at Kimmy, and she had a huge grin spread across her face. The song went really well, and even though the crowd wasn't huge, they applauded enthusiasti-

cally when we finished. For our next number we
did a slow country ballad by Vince Gill, "When
I Call Your Name." We'd never done it in public
before, but we'd worked really hard on the harmonies for the chorus. The verses I sang alone,
closing my eyes and wailing into my vocal mike.
We sounded so good together—the blend of our
voices, the feel we had for each other and the
music. How could Trey have said Wild Hearts
was second-rate? Was it possible that he was
wrong?

We finished the song to major applause and
then launched right into "Down at the Twist and
Shout," by Mary-Chapin Carpenter. It's super
upbeat and we were having a great time, when
out of the corner of my eye I caught a familiar
face.

Wyatt Shane.

He was standing there with his girlfriend,
Brenda Pirkell, an Amazon who had tried to beat
Jane up when she thought Jane was after Wyatt.

Wyatt Shane is lower than the lowest, and he
thinks he is God's gift to girls. If that isn't bad
enough, he hates all of us in Wild Hearts and
would probably do just about anything to hurt
us. His arm was still in a cast from his drunk-
driving accident with Jane's mother's car.

"You suck!" Wyatt yelled up at us through his
cupped hands.

Brenda snorted and fell all over herself, as if Wyatt had said something unbearably witty.

I caught Kimmy's eye, but we ignored Wyatt and just kept singing and playing. By the time we finished the song it was raining steadily, and not too many people were still watching us. The stage was under an awning, but still, we were freezing. The few people who were left applauded us.

Brenda held a newspaper over Wyatt's head so he wouldn't get wet—couldn't you just hurl?—and Wyatt yelled up at us again. "Cover tunes are boring! Get off the stage!"

Sandra walked over to me. "How about if I clobber him with my bass?"

"Why wreck a perfectly good guitar?" I responded.

"You suck!" Wyatt yelled again into his cupped hands.

I felt so powerful—it was the speed. I jumped up from the piano and walked to the apron of the stage, rain streaming down on me. "Listen, you bastard," I hissed, "get the hell away from us. Get a life, get an IQ, or just plain *get!*"

For just a second Wyatt looked shocked. I mean, I am not known for my nasty mouth. That was more Jane's department.

"Oh, yeah, who's gonna make me?" Wyatt finally shot back.

"I am, you low-life scum bucket from hell! You make me sick! You disgust me!" I yelled to him again.

Sandra walked over to me and touched my arm lightly. "Hey, Savy, chill," she murmured.

Wyatt and Brenda both made a totally rude gesture, like the cretins they are.

I shook off Sandra and was ready to catapult myself off the stage to beat both of their smug faces with my fists.

The two dozen or so people who were still watching us perform looked up at me curiously. Blood pounded in my ears. My heart was racing.

"Uh, miss?" the MC said, walking over to me. "We're going to close the stage down until it stops raining. I'm about to make an announcement."

I tore my eyes from Wyatt and stepped back under the awning as the woman went to the mike to tell what few people were left that we were closing down.

I walked off with my friends into the small dressing-room area that had been set up.

"Savy?" Kimmy said, a look of real concern on her face. "Are you okay?"

"Sure," I said. But I couldn't sit still. I paced across the tiny room. I hated the way I felt— angry, out of control, like I could have jumped out of my own skin.

Sandra put her hands on her hips and looked me dead in the eye. "Are you on something?"

"Yeah, right," I snorted. "I don't do drugs."

Jane came up next to Sandra. "There's a first time for everything," she said dryly. "You are acting major bizarro."

"Why, because I stuck up for the band?" I asked Jane. I impatiently swept some of the wet hair off my face. "Wyatt Shane deserves to get his ass kicked."

"Oh, and I guess you're the woman to do it— all five feet two inches of you," Sandra commented.

"Just leave me alone," I snapped, and began pacing again. I knew I was acting weird, but I just couldn't help myself.

Kimmy touched my arm. "Savy? Please, talk to me."

"I'm fine," I insisted, still pacing.

"You're not fine," Kimmy said.

"Look, Kimmy, we're not ten years old anymore, okay?" I blasted at her. "We don't tell each other every time we burp, okay?"

She took a step away from me. "I don't know what's going on with you," she said, her eyes filling up with tears. "I don't even know who you are right now."

"Savy, we are not stupid," Sandra said.

"What did you do, coke or speed?" Jane asked.

"Nothing," I still insisted. I looked at my watch. It was almost ten-thirty. I looked around for my purse. "I gotta go."

"Woah, there," Jane said. "You can't go. If the rain slows down, we're back on."

"I'm not," I said. "I gotta go." I found my purse and slung the strap over my shoulder. Then I picked up my overnight bag that had the hideous pink dress and heels in it.

Somehow the bag had come unzipped. I picked it up upside down, and the pink dress and heels came tumbling out.

I bent down to pick it up, and the empty vial from the little red pills fell out of my pocket.

Sandra picked it up. She held it up to me. Sandra, Jane, and Kimmy all stood there staring at me.

"Okay, so I took a little speed," I said, holding the pink outfit in my hand. "It's not such a big deal."

"But you hate drugs!" Kimmy cried.

"That isn't a drug. It's just to give me a little energy," I explained.

"You know, my mom still has this old button she used to wear in the seventies," Sandra said. "It says 'Speed kills.' "

I sighed dramatically. "Do I look like a speed freak to you?"

"Not yet," Sandra said pointedly.

"And where are you going with that tacky little pink number and the seriously out-of-date heels?" Jane asked me, looking at the stuff in my hands.

"To sing, okay?" I blurted out. I just couldn't take another minute of this interrogation. "I'm singing for the head of Avalon Records tonight at Derek's Corner."

They were all quiet for a moment.

"Without us?" Kimmy finally said.

"Why should you care?" I snapped at her. "You were ready to quit this band until Sawyer opened his mouth and suggested maybe you should stay in it."

"I think maybe we have some things to talk about," Sandra said quietly.

"Well, I don't have time for a postmortem right now. I gotta go."

I hated the look of betrayal on their faces. And at that moment I wanted nothing more than to stay there with my friends, to have everything be the way it used to be.

But it was too late.

I ran.

"You're late," Trey said as he slammed the door of the taxi I'd just gotten out of. He had been waiting for me in front of Derek's Corner.

"I got held up," I explained evasively.

He hustled me into the club and back to the little dressing-room area. A number of different musicians were milling about, some singing snatches of songs, some tuning guitars, others laughing and joking with each other.

"Will your hair fluff up?" Trey asked me nervously, feeling the sodden ends gingerly.

"Yes, just let me go change," I said irritably. I felt pushed and pulled from all directions. I grabbed my stuff and slammed into the ladies' room.

Quickly I pulled off my Wild Hearts outfit—black jeans, flannel shirt, and black suede fringed vest, and pulled the hideous pink thing over my head. Then I pulled off my cowboy boots, pulled on some pantyhose, and stepped into the pink pumps.

Two girls in jeans and T-shirts stared at me when I came out of the stall.

Well, of course. No one dressed like this at a showcase club.

I fixed my bedraggled makeup as best as I could, then went to find Trey.

He wasn't in the dressing room. Instead I found Ryan, munching on a package of cheese crackers and peanut butter. He had on jeans and a black long-sleeved T-shirt, and he had a flannel shirt tied around his waist. He looked cute and comfortable, which was more than I could say for myself.

"You're eating every time I see you," I said, stuffing my suitcase in the corner under a chair.

"Well, hi," he said, "nice to see you, too." He dropped his long body onto a tiny chair and gave me a funny look. "What are you wearing?"

"A dress. I'm sure you've heard of them."

"Yeah," Ryan agreed, "but they usually leave more to the imagination than that one." He held out the crackers to me.

I shook my head and tried to fluff up my still wet hair. "Trey picked it out," I admitted.

"Figures," Ryan mumbled.

I put my hands on my hips. "What is that supposed to mean?"

Two guys carrying acoustic guitars came into the dressing room. They gave me that once-over look that I hate. I tugged down the bottom of the dress self-consciously. "Where's Trey?" I asked Ryan.

"Probably out bribing the guy from Avalon," Ryan said ironically.

I ignored Ryan and walked out into the back of the club, searching through the dark room for Trey. The room was filling up, and my heart began to hammer. This was my big chance. I had to be wonderful.

I went back to the dressing room and paced back and forth nervously. My hands were sweating, and I bit anxiously at my lower lip.

"Hey, you're gonna wear a groove in that floor pacing like that," Ryan said.

"I'm a little nervous," I admitted. I made myself sit down, but I couldn't stand being still, and I quickly jumped up again. For a moment I felt dizzy and woozy, but the feeling passed. "Where's Carl and Pete?" I asked. Pete was Jack Flash's lead guitar player, and Carl played the drums.

"Out there with some girls, as usual," Ryan said, watching me pace. He scrutinized me. "You look skinny," he said.

"Thanks," I replied.

"I didn't mean it as a compliment," Ryan said. "I meant it as an observation." He kept studying me.

"Look, take a picture, it'll last longer," I finally snapped.

Finally he sat up straight and snapped his fingers. "Hey, now I know who you remind me of! Krissy!"

I stopped pacing and turned to him. "What did you say?"

"She had a dress almost exactly like that, only red!" Ryan said. "Trey got it for her!"

"So? Maybe he likes this style."

Ryan got up slowly and walked over to me. He peered into my eyes.

"What?" I finally asked with irritation.

"Your pupils are the size of pinpricks," he said in a low voice. "You did some speed, didn't you?"

I turned away without answering him.

"Jesus, he's doing it again!" Ryan cried bitterly.

I turned around. "What are you talking about?"

"Oh, man, how could I have been so stupid?" he asked, smacking himself in the forehead. He grabbed my arm and pulled me down into a chair next to him. "Listen to me, Savy. You've got to get away from Trey."

"What are you talking about?" I tried to jump up, but Ryan's strong arms pulled me down.

"He's gonna ruin you the same way he ruined Krissy," Ryan said intensely.

I laughed, but even to my own ears my laugh sounded weird and out of control. "Don't you have that a little backwards?" I asked him. "Trey made Krissy's career, and Krissy blew it with drugs and alcohol."

"Savy, that isn't true," Ryan insisted in a low, earnest voice. "Yeah, when Trey met Krissy, she drank too much, but she never drank onstage and she never drank at rehearsal. Then he got ahold of her. Nothing she did was good enough. She wasn't pretty enough or thin enough—"

"Krissy was like a skeleton!" I objected.

"Not when we started," Ryan said. "She was normal, healthy-looking. But Trey convinced her she was fat. Even after she lost all that weight, he always told her she was five pounds from perfection. Then he convinced her she wasn't working hard enough, that she didn't have what it took to do the job. So he gave her some little red pills to give her more energy—"

This time I did jump up, my heart beating so wildly I thought it would fly out of my chest. The dizziness came over me again, but I shook it off. "That is a big lie!" I yelled.

Ryan stood up and grabbed my arm. "It's not a lie," he insisted. "Trey kept her supplied with speed, and she lost more and more weight. She couldn't sleep, so she started drinking more and more to knock herself out at night. He made her over, put her in skimpy, stupid outfits like the one you have on right now, tried to sell her as this sex queen, but that wasn't Krissy. She always felt like a fraud, and the worse she felt, the more dependent she got on pills and booze—"

"I don't believe you!" I screamed.

"Believe me," Ryan said. "Please believe me. Trey is sick, Savy. He's a user. He's super-insecure, I guess, and he hates himself. Then he projects that hate onto someone else—Krissy, you. . . . You're never gonna be good enough or pretty enough or thin enough to suit him. He'll use you until he uses you up, and then he'll find a new victim."

"No," I whimpered.

"Yes," Ryan insisted. "I didn't even see the whole thing myself until now. God, I've been such a butt-head! I let him do it to Krissy because he was getting us so much work. I . . . I looked the other way. But I can't let him do it to you, too!"

I pulled away from his grasp, turned, and went running into the club, wobbling around on those stupid high heels.

But where could I run to when something in my heart told me that Ryan was telling me the truth?

Then I saw Trey, separating himself from a group at a big table, coming toward me. At the same time, Ryan came out of the dressing room looking for me.

Suddenly my vision got blurry. My heart was pounding so hard I thought I might have a heart attack. Then the room seemed to be sliding, slipping, as if it were melting. I grabbed at the air, at nothing, and I was falling, falling, falling. . . .

And that's the last thing I remember.

CHAPTER
14

❤️

I woke up with a bunch of faces looming over me—Ryan, Kimmy, Jane, and Sandra.

I started to sit up, but Ryan's hand gently pushed me back down.

"Take it easy," he said.

"Here, this'll help," Kimmy said in her soft voice. She put a pillow under my head and straightened the itchy blanket that covered my legs.

I refused to say "Where am I?" because it seemed too much like a line from a really bad movie, so I just took a minute to figure it out for myself. I was in the back of Jack Flash's van. Ryan and my friends were all sitting around me.

My friends. My friends who probably hated my guts by now. I remembered everything that had happened that night and closed my eyes again.

"How are you feeling?" Kimmy asked me.

"Awful," I said honestly. "How did ya'll get here?" I thought about this a minute. "And where *is* here, anyway?"

"We're in the parking lot at Derek's Corner," Ryan explained. "I carried you out the back way so we wouldn't create a major scene."

"How long ago was that?" I asked him.

"Just a few minutes," he replied. "Your friends just got here—they told me they came over because they were worried about you. I recognized them from the arthritis telethon. We played that gig with Krissy."

"So he called us over to this van," Jane continued, "and we found you lying here like dead meat, dead to the world."

"I figured if you didn't come to right away, I could drive you to the hospital or something," Ryan said.

"I'm fine," I insisted. My friends stared at me. "No, I'm not fine. I feel awful."

"Well, that's the first honest thing you've said in days," Sandra allowed. "You look like hell, I might add."

"When's the last time you ate anything?" Jane asked me.

"I don't remember," I admitted.

Ryan reached into his shirt pocket and pulled out a candy bar. "I'm always prepared."

I grabbed the candy, tore the wrapper open, and took a huge bite. "Mmmm, this is the best thing I ever tasted."

"Why did you stop eating?" Kimmy asked.

"To lose weight," I explained. "I wanted to do it fast and ... Look, it was stupid, okay?" I took another huge bite of the candy bar. "What made ya'll come over here?"

"Because you were acting so bizarre," Jane said. "We were worried about you."

"I'm surprised you're even speaking to me," I said in a low voice.

"Me, too," Sandra agreed. "You were really obnoxious."

"But it wasn't you!" Kimmy protested. "I mean, we all knew it wasn't you! So we had to come see if you were okay!"

I swallowed the last of Ryan's candy bar. "Thanks," I told him in a shaky voice.

"No problem," he said with a grin. "I'm glad you're okay."

This time I did sit up. "Where's Trey? Oh, God, what about the guy from Avalon Records?"

"We missed our time slot," Ryan said with a shrug.

"I'm really sorry," I began, "I—"

"Hey, it's okay," Ryan interrupted me. "According to Trey, the guy was coming to look at you, not the band."

"Well, I guess I blew that," I said with a sigh.

"Hey, it could be worse," Ryan said. "You could have gone onstage in that pink thing and then fainted in front of everybody."

"We're talking major flashing in that little number," Jane added.

"Does Trey know?" I asked Ryan.

Ryan nodded. "He saw me carrying you out. I told him that you knew everything, the whole truth about Krissy. He just swore a blue streak at me and said I'd better watch my ass, 'cuz he was gonna get me."

I felt so sad. "I thought he cared about me. I can't believe I trusted him."

Ryan smoothed hair off my face. "I trusted him once, too, Savy. Don't be too hard on yourself. So, listen, I'm gonna go in and see what's up with the band and everything. You'll be okay?"

I nodded. "Ryan?"

He turned to me.

"Thanks," I whispered.

And then, in front of all my friends, Ryan Black leaned over and kissed me on the lips. "You haven't seen the last of me," he promised, and then he jumped out of the van.

"He wants you bad," Jane said in a teasing voice.

"He's a good guy," I replied, "and I completely overlooked him before." I glanced around at the concerned expressions on my friends' faces. "Listen, ya'll, I messed up big-time."

"That's true," Jane agreed. "I mean, speed? Bogus drug, Savy."

"And lying to us," Sandra added. "That was low."

"It was," Kimmy agreed, "and you used me so you could be with Trey!"

"Hey, wait a sec!" I cried. "Let's take some time out here before the three of you get all self-righteous! Ya'll were putting everything else before Wild Hearts—tennis, work, and guys," I added pointedly, looking at Kimmy.

In the glow from the parking-lot lights shining into the van I could see that she was blushing.

"We all agreed we were only going to do the band if it could be first-rate," I continued. "But stuff kept getting in the way. I was so angry—"

"So why didn't you tell us?" Jane asked.

"I did!" I insisted. "But no one was listening to me!"

"You didn't talk to me," Kimmy said softly. "You shut me out completely."

"That is just not true," I protested. "You became this space cadet, only interested in Sawyer. He was everything, and I was nothing!"

"Oh, Savy, that's not true! You're my best friend in the entire world, and you always will be!"

"Well, that's not how it felt," I replied. "You got all ... all icky about him. I felt so sad, like we would never be the same again."

"Maybe I did go a little overboard," Kimmy allowed.

"A little?" Jane snorted. "You have been, like, *drowning* in the guy!"

"I guess because I couldn't believe that a guy like Sawyer could really like me," Kimmy admitted.

"Well, he does," I reminded her. "But if you change yourself into some kind of ... Pastel Person whose life revolves around him, you won't be the girl he fell for anymore."

Kimmy nodded. "I'm beginning to see that. I think that's why he encouraged me to stay in Wild Hearts."

"Well, I don't know if there still *is* a Wild Hearts," Sandra said.

I looked at her. "Did I ruin everything?"

She sighed. "I don't know. But I don't want to go through all this trauma every time we have a problem, you know? We've got to be honest with each other."

"You're right," I agreed. "I know you're right." I looked at my watch. "I'm gonna go in and deal with Trey, if he's in there," I said.

"You want moral support?" Jane asked me.

I smiled at her gratefully. "Yeah."

We got out of the van—fortunately it had stopped raining—and went into the club. Almost immediately Trey came rushing over.

"I can't believe you blew tonight," he said in a low voice.

"I fainted," I told him. "I fainted from not eating and doing the speed you gave me."

"You're a big girl," Trey said coldly. "You should be able to monitor your own health, you know?"

"No, I guess I don't know," I said. "I want to know if what Ryan told me is true. Did you give Krissy speed because you told her she was fat?"

"She needed to lose a little weight."

"Just like I did?" I asked him.

"Well, you did," he insisted. "I did it for you."

"You did it for yourself," I said.

He shook his head at me. "Man, you are all alike. You can't take the heat, and you blame everything on me. You've got a real problem, Savy."

"No, I don't have a problem," I corrected him. "You have a problem. And you're no longer my manager."

He laughed. "Yeah, like I care. I only pretended to like you, you know. I never really gave a damn about you. Some little sixteen-year-old fat girl? Gimme a break! You and your crappy little teeny-bopper girls' band deserve each other! Ya'll suck!"

At that moment Sandra stepped around me, pulled her fist back, and punched Trey in the nose.

"Hey!" he screeched. "I think you broke my nose! Hey!"

But we didn't pay any attention. The girls of Wild Hearts just turned around, and together we walked out the door.

"Goodness, gracious, Great Balls of Fire!"

We had all gone back to my house, and we'd gravitated down to the music room where we'd all spent so many hours working on the band. I had grabbed a sandwich on my way through the kitchen and gobbled it ravenously. Then we started playing "Great Balls of Fire," singing and dancing around the room.

There was no feeling to compare to it. It was the greatest, a natural high, much better than the way I'd felt after swallowing the evil little red pills. How could I have been so stupid as to risk what I cared about the most?

"Ya'll, listen," I said, when we brought the song to a close. "I was an idiot, okay?"

They all nodded.

"I'm not gonna lie to ya'll anymore or hide things or ... or be so inflexible when ya'll have other commitments—"

"Please," Sandra cautioned with a laugh, "don't get that perfect. The rest of us could never live up to it!"

"I'm just trying to say that I'm sorry," I said simply.

"Me, too," Kimmy said. "I got kind of carried away with Sawyer, huh?"

"Well, I'm not apologizing for having to slave at Uncle Zap's," Jane said. "And I'm not apologizing for taking time to work against those cretins who wanted to ban books. I mean, life is too short!"

"It can't all be music, is that what you're saying," I interpreted, swinging around on the piano bench.

"Yeah, right," Jane agreed. "Music is the most important thing, but it can't be the only thing."

Sandra looked at me. "Can you live with that?"

I looked around at my friends. They were so great. "Yeah, I can live with that," I finally said.

"Well, good," Sandra said. "Then we're cool."

She started playing a riff on her bass, the very recognizable line we used to begin "It Wasn't God Who Made Honky Tonk Angels," which was our signature song. I came in on the piano, Kimmy added the guitar, and Jane came in on the drums. We sang in tight four-part harmony, rocking out to the country classic.

When we finished, I heard applause from the doorway.

"Hotter than a pistol!" my dad said. He had a grin on his face, but I noticed something in his eyes that didn't look right, though.

"Ya'll sounded great," my mother added.

"Want to come play with us?" I asked impetuously.

"Oh, no," my dad demurred. "It's really late."

"Come on!" I wheedled. Suddenly I was in such a wonderful mood that I wanted to share it with my whole family. And even though it was so late at night, no one had to get up in the morning. At my house we'd been known to stay up playing music on a Saturday until the wee hours of the morning.

I grabbed my mom by one hand and my dad by the other. "We'll do a bunch of country standards and drive Jane up the wall."

"No, honey," my mom said, hanging back.

"Well, you know Gramma Beth can talk ya'll

into it," I said with a grin. "Let's go ambush her and get her down here with her fiddle ..."

I saw a shadow cross over my father's face, something that made me feel suddenly cold.

"Gramma Beth isn't here, honey," my father said.

"I thought she was supposed to get home from the fiddlers' convention today," I said.

My parents exchanged that funny look they'd been trading for days.

"She didn't go to a fiddlers' convention," my mother said slowly.

"So where is she, then?" I asked, not sure I really wanted to know.

A muscle twitched near my father's mouth. "She's in the hospital, honey. At Vanderbilt."

Dread clutched at my heart like a hurting fist. "But why?" I whispered. "Nothing is wrong with Gramma Beth."

"She's been having bad headaches for weeks, honey," my mother said gently. "She's in the hospital having tests. The doctors think she might have a brain tumor."

"No," I whispered.

"It's okay, honey," my mother said, putting her arm around me.

"No..." I insisted. I realized dimly that Kimmy, Sandra, and Jane had all moved in next to me, that Kimmy had her hand in mine, that Jane and Sandra were both touching my arm.

"But ... she lied to me," I whispered. "You all lied to me!"

"To protect you," my father said.

I put my hand over my mouth. Lies were so awful. When I told them to my friends. When my family told them to me. Lying didn't change the hurt; it just made it feel like more of a betrayal.

"Is she ...Will she ..." I stammered. I couldn't bear to ask if Gramma Beth would be okay, if she would even live.

"They have to repeat some tests and then decide if they're going to operate," my father said. "We just don't know very much yet."

"I want to see her," I said firmly.

"Yes, she wants to see you, too," my mother said.

"So do I," Kimmy piped up.

"Me, too," Jane added.

"Me, too," Sandra said.

My parents smiled at us.

"Ya'll can go over to the hospital tomorrow," my father said. "You can't all go in at once, though."

"We'll go with you, Savy," Kimmy promised.

Jane and Sandra nodded.

"We'll take her some music," Sandra suggested. "I've got a great Mark O'Connor fiddle tape."

"Oh, let's tape some Wild Hearts stuff for her!" Jane suggested. "She'll love that!"

Tears came to my eyes. Everything felt scary. But there I was, surrounded by Kimmy and Jane and Sandra, with my parents standing nearby. I wouldn't fall apart. I would be strong for Gramma Beth, just as she had always been strong for me.

"Let's practice," I said firmly, swallowing my tears.

You might prefer the Whitney Houston version—the one from *The Bodyguard*—but it was Dolly Parton who was singing in my ear as I headed back over to my piano, as the music grew louder, lifting me up, making me strong.

"I Will Always Love You . . ."

Heart to Heart
~ ♥ ♥ ~

Dear Cherie,

I absolutely adored your new book, WILD HEARTS ON FIRE! I thought it was hilarious as well as emotional. I really got a feel for each of the characters. I especially enjoyed Kimmy's make-over ... and the suspense, wondering if Dave really was going to pull the trigger. This was all around a great, wonderful, awesome, spectacular, superb and dazzling book of magnificent brilliance!! I give it four thumbs up! I'm definitely going to follow the WILD HEARTS series as well as the SUNSET ISLAND series. They're both well worth it! WILD HEARTS RULE!

> *Sincerely, The Biggest Cherie Bennett Fan*
> *You Could Possibly Imagine,*
> *Kim Hargrave*
> *Fullerton, CA*

Dear Kim,

Woah, baby, I guess this means you really liked the book! You know, being a writer is

ary thing. I mean, here I sit,
our at my computer, and some-
ll . . . kind of lonely! So when
I get a letter like yours it makes me feel
really terrific. It was interesting writing
about someone like Dave Mallone. I've
never actually known anyone who went off
quite like he does in WILD HEARTS ON
FIRE, but I do remember how my brother,
Steve, was considered dweeby in high
school, and how mean some kids were to
him. That kind of thing really hurts, you
know? Why do you think some kids feel
they have to put down others? Any ideas
out there? And what can we do about it?

Best,
Cherie

Dear Cherie,

*I was so excited to read WILD HEARTS ON
FIRE. It is an excellent book. It was exciting and
full of surprises. Since my dad lives in Nashville
it was cool knowing where the girls lived and
places they talked about. This book was great all
the way through. I couldn't put it down. The way
the end turned out was really very shocking. An-*

other reason I like the four girls is because I'm like all of them in some ways, so it's easy to relate!

> *Sincerely,*
> *Leah Peterzell*
> *Knoxville, TN*

Dear Leah,

It was interesting to hear that you can relate to all four girls, because I can, too! At times I've been as sarcastic as Jane, as insecure as Kimmy, as enthusiastic as Savy and as practical as Sandra. But who am I the most like? I guess I'd have to say Jane—although I can't say I've ever dressed like her! Who do the rest of you out there most relate to?

> Best,
> Cherie

Dear Cherie,

I just finished reading WILD HEARTS. You really outdid yourself this time. I can't wait for the next book to come out. I really do like all four of the girls in the band, but I have to say that Savy and Jane are my favorites. Wyatt really did sound like a slimeball! I thought it was great that people wanted to sue him for his stupidity!

Your fan,
Adreana Michelle Frost
Flora Vista, NM

Dear Adreana,

I think Wyatt is a slimeball, too! But you know, I think every girl falls for a great-looking slimeball at least once in her life. For me it was Joel Lansit, and I was in the eighth grade. He was totally gorgeous and had the brain of a turnip. He was seriously in love with his own reflection. But did I notice? I did not. I checked my brains at the door there for about three months and spent most of my time either with him, day-dreaming about him, or writing his name over and over in my journal. Naturally he eventually broke my heart. Hey, I'm older and wiser now, and married to Mr. Wonderful. I wonder what ever happened to Joel? And how many of you out there have ever fallen for a guy who turned out to be totally unworthy of your time and affection?

Best,
Cherie

Dear Readers,

Howdy, how's it going, what's happening, and all that? I really enjoyed writing this particular WILD HEARTS book, because I remember what it felt like to have a guy who seemed to be really cool try to change me into what he wanted me to be. And you know, it's so hard to believe in yourself enough to stand up to that kind of pressure, know what I mean? I also remember what it felt like to have my best friend fall in love when I didn't even have a boyfriend. Only in my case, my best friend fell in love with . . . *my older brother!!* Now, *that* was excruciating! One night she came to my house for a sleepover, but then ended up spending all her time with my brother. I got so jealous that I threw all her clothes down the stairs. Okay, I'm not proud of that. Have any of you had any experience with this? How did you handle it?

I have been getting the most wonderful mail from you WILD HEARTS out there! Keep those cards and letters coming, okay? Send me your photo, too, and I'll put it up in my office, which is literally covered with photos of my readers.

And let me tell you, you guys are soooo cute! I will continue to personally answer each and every letter I receive—I won't let you down. Just let me know if I can consider your letter for publication or if it's private.

So, Cherie, babe, what's the next WILD HEARTS book and when can I get it? you ask. The next book is WILD HEARTS ON THE EDGE, out in late July. If you've ever had problems with a parent or a boyfriend who didn't support what is important to you, you'll relate to this one!

Thank you, thank you, thank you for being the greatest fans in the world. I'll keep writing as long as you keep reading.

Wild Hearts forever!

Cherie Bennett

Cherie Bennett
c/o Archway Paperbacks
Pocket Books
1230 Avenue of the Americas
New York, NY 10020

About the Author

Cherie Bennett is one of the bestselling novelists for young adults in North America. She is also an award-winning playwright and screenwriter. She is married to theatre and film producer Jeff Gottesfeld. They live in Nashville, Tennessee.